ERIN BUTLER

Evernight Teen

www.evernightteen.com

AUTHOR NOTE

The witch in *BLOOD HEX* is based on 16th century prophetess Mother Shipton.

ERIN BUTLER

DEDICATION

For Grandma & Grandpa

ACKNOWLEDGMENTS

As a writer, you get excited over little things like your first "Acknowledgments", but wow, these things are really hard, so here goes! (If I forget anybody, blame it on the jitters.)

To my family—Mom, Dad, Sar, Rich—I'm not even sure I know what to say. All four of you have probably felt like killing me at some point in my life, but I'm very glad you didn't. Thank you for not getting too mad when I'd rather spend time alone dreaming about people who don't exist. Thank you for understanding when I choose to write instead of going out to breakfast, or talk on the phone with you. Thank you for being there for me. Always. I love you.

To my husband, Tommy—I'm glad you don't care that your wife is pretty much useless at being a wife. Maybe in my next life I won't loathe cooking, but probably not. Thank you for encouraging me every single day, for talking me out of my funks, for doing the dishes so I won't feel so bad about letting the house go to crap while I'm writing. But most of all, thank you for allowing me to do this writing thing. I love you very much.

To Grandma and Grandpa—I dedicated this book to you because I'm not sure it would even exist had you guys not been in my life and then taken from it too early. I miss you guys every day. Every. Day.

To Aunt Mary—I got my awesome taste in music and my love of books from you. You probably didn't know how much books would influence my life when you passed, but I hope you do now. Thank you for everything. I hope I am half the aunt you were.

To Tyler—One day you WILL read this book. And when you do, I hope you like it.

To my nieces, (because God knows I will probably never have kids) Abby, Payten, and Riley—Don't ever let anyone tell you you can't do something. I mean it. When you get older, you'll find something that you want more than anything else in the world. Follow those dreams. They can come true.

And to the rest of my entire family—Thank you for talking to me about my writing, about my books, for being excited when I told you I was getting published. And thank you to those who read the earlier versions of this story and didn't laugh.

To friends on QT—I learned a lot here. Thanks to those who helped me with my query, my first pages, and to those who read parts of *Blood Hex* and offered me tips and advice on my writing. And to Kimmy, thank you for talking me off a few ledges while I queried publishers with this book.

And finally, to Evernight Teen—I'm so glad you wanted to publish *Blood Hex*. Thank you to my editor for helping me whip the story into shape, and thank you to marketing for helping get the word out.

ERIN BUTLER

BLOOD HEX

Erin Butler

Copyright © 2013

Chapter One

Present Day

After 900 miles, my hands should have been sure on the steering wheel, but they shook like prisoners' hands against their cages. I curled them under to release the tension. It didn't work. Nothing worked.

In the darkness of the car, with the radio off, I tried to hold a picture in my mind of what would happen. Imagine the different scenarios. I'd had two days to prepare for this after all. Two days of staring at a double solid yellow line, of stopping at gross, backwoods gas stations to pee, of watching the tree-lined highway blur into streaking greens.

The drive seemed like only seconds now that I was here. *How could I have driven for two days and not come up with a plan, an escape route, or...I don't know, which greeting I should use? Hello? Hey? What's up?*

I suck at life. Obviously.

Now that I was one step away, I could truly let myself believe in this moment. Except at this moment, both my body and my mind wouldn't anchor down. Insane thought after insane thought swirled around inside, making me feel as if I sailed the deep, rough waters of the Atlantic in a rowboat without any motion sickness pills.

I managed to turn into the circular driveway, grip stumbling along the wheel as the GPS's tinny, indifferent voice announced, "You have reached your destination."

Outside, the trees bowed with the weight of the wind, the leaves displayed their bellies in a twisting dance for the moonlight. The house rose up like a statue. Big, foreign, a secluded shadow in a clump of old maples, a sentinel towering over the encroaching forest. The windows and roofs peaked at different heights and different angles, each adorned with intricate woodwork. The house may have been beautiful a hundred, maybe even fifty years ago, but even in the dark, I could see cracked white paint and broken molding.

One of the first floor windows held the only sign of life. Streams of different colors played out on the paned glass, blues and reds. Then a bright white flashed erratically before dimming to black. I crouched over the wheel. An old TV set, the kind framed in wood, sat along the far wall of the room.

"Well, we're here." We. Like someone else cared enough to make the journey. Whatever. I was used to being on my own.

The clock in the dash read 10:30. Lovely. Time went by like warp speed today. Being on the road was like being in another dimension. There were never enough minutes for the miles I put in between here and home and definitely not enough miles between Mom and me.

My skin pricked. I wouldn't enjoy what I had to do next. Maybe. I let a smile creep onto my lips. However, it was a means to an end. The finale before the beginning. The meal before a chocolate dessert. I just wished it didn't involve speaking to my mother.

I thrummed my fingers against my thigh trying to think of an out. Then, after taking a long look over at the passenger seat and the brown leather book lying there, I yelled at myself, "Don't. Wimp. Out. Now." Finally, I reached out and hit the call button. It beeped, waiting for direction. "Call Mom."

The car's Bluetooth dialed and then rang. Loud music and the cackle of Mom's exaggerated laughter belted out of the speakers. It was one of her old tricks, no doubt fueled by her next conquest. The higher the laugh, the more she wanted to impress. And what, she had been single for almost two weeks now? So yeah, it was time. "Hel-lo," Mom shouted, voice dripping with alcohol. "What's up girlfriend?"

"I asked you not to call me that."

"What-ever," she crooned. A male's husky laugh erupted over the speaker. *He must be loaded. She's on fire tonight.*

I couldn't resist an eye roll, though it always got a better reaction when I was actually in the same vicinity as Cici. Of course, I did get pleasure out of knowing I got away with one without having to hear, 'You'd better roll those eyes right back to the beginning.' "You realize it's Tuesday, right?"

"Of course I know it's Tuesday. Fat Tuesday! I'm at the Clamshell!" The speaker bounced the shrill voice around the interior of the car before giggles took over.

I careened my head. There was no getting away. Three states in between us and still trapped.

Two nights ago, the same ensnared feeling choked me. Mom came home after a late night out, not caring I already lay in bed asleep. Could have been the same guy she flirted with tonight, but my educated guess—and I was usually right—it was a totally different guy. They probably dressed the same, had the same gelled hair and roughly the same amount of money in their savings CD's, but they were different. Different color hair. Different color eyes. Different name. Different opinions on Cici having a grown, teenage daughter.

Unrestrained laughter—and a male's to match—strangled me through the floorboards at two in the morning. I freakin' lost it. Marching right across the hall to my mother's room, I started tearing at things.

The dresser first. When finished, I smiled down at a rainbow of undergarments littering the four-poster bed. Then, I moved to the closet. An old shoebox I flung to the opposite side of the room spilled open. The corner of a brown leather book peeked out. I picked up the journal, expecting it to be Cici's. It wasn't. I was disappointed at first; thinking posting her diary all over Facebook would be more than a little awesome.

What I found meant more than that. I decided then I'd had enough.

Done. Finito. The end.

Now, all this physical distance between us and we still played the same old games. Except for this time, I held all the ammunition. Electricity burned through me with a mash of excitement and anger. "Well, I'm here, Mom."

"Here? The Clamshell? Where are you? We'll come say hey."

Yeah. Right. "No. Mom, I'm in Adams." I paused, waiting for the name to resonate. Waiting for a tiny, little light bulb to go off in her head. Apparently, the alcohol numbed her memories along with her speaking ability because she didn't say anything. So I said, "Virginia."

"You're where? You're breaking up." Other than the throbbing of the house music behind Mom's slurring, the sound was like crystal. Clear enough to hear her whisper, "One sec," to the next poor, unknowing target.

I sighed, realizing this conversation headed nowhere. As usual. Boredom had already moved into Cici's brain and set up shop. I pictured her cozying up next to this guy on one of the brown leather couches at The Clamshell, covering up the speaker on her cell and promising to get rid of her annoying daughter as soon as possible. She wanted to get back to her *guy friend,* as she always called them. Glad to know I'm missed. "I'm at Rose McCallister's house," I said, speaking slow, deliberate.

"Who's that? Are you okay? Do you need a ride?"

I lost her already. She wasn't even listening anymore. "Not unless you want to come nine-hundred miles to pick me up. Besides, you already know who Rose is."

"Huh? Where are you again?" Cici's voice sobered in an instant, proving what I always believed. Mom lived the life of a con artist. Faker. Liar. Whatever you wanted to call it. If she acted vulnerable enough, she could trap anyone.

"I found Dad's journal."

Cici made the annoyed guttural sound she always did when she had to "deal" with her hormonal teenage daughter. "Can this wait until we get home?"

"It'll be pretty hard to do that since I'm not coming home."

"Huh? Sarah, you're not making any sense. I'll be home in a little while." She sighed. "Listen, I'll stop by the Bucks, get you a mochachino, and then we'll sit out on the patio and have a nice chat." There it was. The mom-of-the-year voice.

"It's too late for that. You lied to me. You've *been* lying to me."

The phone muffled for a second. It sounded like Cici said, "Teenagers…" to her guy friend. Teenagers, like the word stank of garbage. Like that one word encapsulated our entire relationship.

The thump, thump of the bass quieted and an echo of a pair of heels bouncing off walls sounded in my ear. I took a deep breath and started in again. "Out of all those times I asked you about Dad, you lied. You lied to me, Mom." I sounded desperate. At this point, I really didn't care. What was it going to take for her to realize how much she hurt me? I blinked away the heat from behind my eyes and pushed a level breath out of my lungs. "I found his journal in your closet," I finally said. The drive, the distance between us, hadn't muted my initial freak out. It fueled it.

I was glad. She deserved it. A piece of paper told me I had family. Not a soft, caressing mother's voice, but a lined piece of journal paper.

"Here we go again." Mom giggled. "You're something else, you know that? You barely even knew him and you like him better than me."

"Give me a reason not to. And besides, this is not about you. It's not always about you." I sucked in air. "Have you even noticed I've been gone for two days? Or have you and Romeo over there been pretty tied up with each other?"

"You watch your mouth," Cici snapped. A faucet turned on and I heard the splash of the water hit the sink. "Let's just both calm down. I will talk to you about this later when I get home."

Again, I spoke slow, making it easy for my mom to understand. To realize this was real, serious, and indeed happening right now. "I'm not home now and I'm not coming home later either."

"Then I'll pick you up at Jaime's." Cici's voice tinged in amusement. "I'll drag you out of there kicking and screaming if I have to."

"I'm not at Jaime's. Aren't you listening? I'm not even in Florida anymore."

"Where are you?"

"I already told you. I'm at dad's aunt's house." I smacked the End button with my palm. The Bluetooth beeped…beeped…beeped. Silence.

Inside, the car felt heavy, empty, and the sigh I expelled from my chest stirred the stagnant air.

****

Rose answered the door in a bathrobe and wire curlers with these pink, plastic, needle-like things struck through them, eyes practically crossed with sleep.

Awesome first impression.

She wore the same thing now, sitting across from me at a dining room table, except her dark eyes stood out, more lucid, clearer. My art teacher in tenth grade said eyes were reflections of the soul. Mrs. Audrey made our class draw eyes over and over because you couldn't draw a good face without the perfect pair of eyes. First, we drew in pencil, then in coal, and last in watercolor. Eyes were hard. I always got points taken off for drawing eyes with the corners turned down. They looked too sad for Mrs. Audrey.

I tried not to talk as the shock wore off and Rose digested things. Ever so slightly, her eyes turned from cloudy to mirrors. Apparently, she didn't even know I existed.

I suspected as much.

Steam from two cups of coffee curled up between us, carrying the smell of ripe, bitter coffee beans. My great aunt speared the silence with her abrupt manner of talking. "Well, I need to call your mother."

"What? Why? I am who I say I am." I motioned toward my bags still sitting in the foyer. "I brought my birth certificate. You can see it."

"No need. I'm not doubting you're David's. Anyone who knew him can tell you're his daughter." She patted the rollers on her head. "You have the same color brown in your hair. And your hazel eyes. Do they—?" Rose paused and cleared her throat. "Do they change—?"

"—change to amber in the sunlight? Yes." I smiled. "My mom let that slip once."

Rose frowned. "I'm going to have to call her, Sarah." She stumbled over my name, testing it on her tongue and then smiled somewhat sheepishly. She was nice. Straightforward, but nice. I was a fan of people who told the truth.

"Could you not do that?" I winced. "She's kinda melodramatic."

"Seems like you take right after her, showing up here late at night without even a phone call." Rose's eyebrow peaked.

Though she didn't ask a question, the need to answer her, the need to prove I was nothing like my mom, pushed forward. Words rushed from my mouth. "It was a last-minute decision. I was just so mad she didn't tell me I had any other family. Besides," I said, putting on my most trusting face. "I called her when I got here."

Rose sipped her coffee, face immeasurable, though it was the most bitter thing I ever tasted in my life. "I have a few things to say to her so I'm calling her too. I haven't spoken to her in seventeen years. I think it's about time." She handed over a napkin and pen that lay on the table. "Here. Write down the number." Rose tapped the side of her coffee cup with her fingertip. I thought about writing down the wrong number briefly. Very briefly. "You can stay here for tonight. Upstairs, to the right, first door on the left. You look like you could sleep for days. I'll call your mom and we'll talk about it in the morning."

I started to get up, then sat back down again. "Why do you think they never told you about me?"

Rose took a deep, steady breath before trying to answer. "With your mother…" She paused, looking into my eyes. I'm not sure what she saw, but she shook her head. "Never mind. I said we'd talk about it in the morning, we'll talk about it in the morning." She raised her hand and shooed me away, hurrying me toward my bags.

I left the mug there, praying she'd never offer me coffee again and practically ran back to the foyer to grab my luggage and haul it up the stairs. I began to envision long, dizzying chats and hours spent poring over pictures and trips to his high school, favorite hangouts, the grocery store. Anywhere my father went, I wanted to go too. If she wanted to call my mom and sleep on it first, then I guess I had to be okay with that.

The room was large and girly with lace everywhere. Like a princess vomited in every corner. So different from the dark blues and harsh steel colors Mom decorated our house with back home. But that was all arbitrary for now. I had to get down to business.

I eyed the door and then shut it with a bang, positive my aunt could hear that from downstairs. Unless she was deaf of course.

The clock on the nightstand read 11:33. I busied myself for a few minutes, taking out pajamas and laying them on the bed. One of the doors in the room led to a bathroom. I checked myself out in the mirror, rubbed off some of the smeared eye makeup, and ran a brush through my hair. Trust me, it was not pretty.

I'd heard of bed head, not car head. No wonder Rose wanted to talk to my mom. I must have seemed like a complete lunatic, showing up at her house so late at night. She probably wanted to make sure I wasn't on any crazy meds or something, before she officially let me stay.

The clock now read 11:35. Satisfied, I went back to the hallway door and eased it open, listening. My aunt's voice drifted up the stairs, but not quite clear enough for me to hear what she was saying. I tiptoed to the staircase and went down.

About halfway, I heard the older woman speak in the same commanding tone. "You don't think I should have known about a niece? My only family. After David died, I didn't have anybody." A long pause ensued where only the sounds of creaking footsteps and sighs made their way up the staircase. At least I wasn't the only one who found my mother annoying as hell. Maybe Rose rolled her eyes, too. Maybe it was just something about my mom that made people want to roll their eyes. "I'm not sure I will send her home. She wants to stay." Another pause. "She's old enough to make her own decisions." I smiled. This. Was. Awesome. I liked the way this woman thought. "No. She's not going home tonight. I already sent her up to a room and I'm going back to bed now, too. Sarah will call you in the morning."

The phone clicked off and Rose's shadow moved into the foyer. I turned, drowning a surprised cry that threatened my lips, and ran back up the stairs trying to make as little noise as possible. This was so my idea of family. A no-nonsense bad ass.

She hung up on my mother. I mean she actually hung up on my mother. I burst out into a big smile. Too freakin' cool.

****

"Hell, it's 9:30!" I screamed into the lacy pillow. A roaring lawn mower had been driving me crazy for over half an hour. The constant noise made it sound as if they'd cut the grass directly underneath my window a gazillion times.

I need sleep.

A picture popped into my mind of Rose in a bathrobe and curlers driving a huge beast of a lawn mower, commanding and taming the machine like she had with Cici last night. Jumping up, I threw the covers off and ran to the window to see, already smiling in anticipation.

"Holy…mm mmm." It wasn't Rose. Nope. For sure not Rose. I stretched my neck and bumped my head on the windowpane. "Ouch." I rubbed at the blossoming sting and then placed my palms on the warm glass. The real life picture also made me smile.

A guy, about my age, tanned to a deep bronze with a great bod, pushed a mower around a beautiful backyard garden with rows and rows of red roses. He wiped at his face using a shirt and then slung it over his shoulder. My aunt came around the side of the house and pointed at the row next to him. He nodded, his sun-tinted golden brown hair falling into his face before he pushed it back with the shirt hem.

Aunt Rose looked less severe this morning. Dark gray curls, with slivers of white mixed in, framed her face. She wore a typical outfit I'd seen on plenty of late night TV Land reruns. Like *The Brady Bunch* or *The Wonder Years*. A belt cinched together a pair of long blue shorts and she had on a sleeveless white top. The usual mom wear, for TV anyway. Definitely not my mom. If Cici wasn't wearing tight black spandex and showing some cleave, it just wasn't a normal day.

I ran downstairs and stopped outside the dining room to scrunch my hair and twist my shirt into place. On the table, steaming stacks of French toast and pancakes replaced the two coffee cups from last night. Ho-ly crap. Did she actually think I ate this much? I turned to go into the kitchen when the door swung open.

Lawn mower hottie stood in the doorway, his body propping the door open as Rose squeezed through with a glass pitcher in her hands. Her eyes lit. "Oh good, you're awake. Drake, we have a guest this morning." Her voice oozed honey. A sweeter, richer tone than last night. "This is my niece. Well, great niece, Sarah."

His lips and blue eyes smiled. His sandy hair was wind-tossed and oh so adorable. He looked even cuter up close and that was saying a lot. I was used to Miami Beach bodies, so…yeah. "So you're the annoying one with the noise this morning?" I asked. He studied me, confused, and a tiny smile slipped onto my face. "Isn't it a little early to be mowing the lawn?"

"Early? I started at nine," he said, smirking. Tiny lines silhouetted his mouth.

"Exactly my point. Nine is still sleep time, not jump outside in the hot sun and push around a loud mower time."

"I guess I missed that in etiquette class."

Rose's eyes flitted back and forth between us, her skin wrinkling as a small grin spread her lips. "Have a seat. Both of you. I've made a big breakfast for the homecoming of my niece."

Drake glanced over at the older woman, his eyes teasing her. "You make the *best* breakfast, Rose."

She laughed and swatted at his arm. "No, you're not getting out of doing the rest of the lawn."

"Come on. You owe me. You never said you had such a cute niece." He turned toward me now and I matched his smile, but if he expected a shy, country girl's rosy cheeks, he wouldn't get it.

Rose continued her watchful gaze and said, "Well kids, I've already eaten so I'll let you guys have at it." She set the pitcher of orange juice down on the table and walked toward the foyer.

"Wait," I called out, my aunt's words finally registering. Stupid boy smiles, they always got to me. "You sure?" Looked like my visions of long conversations and strolling through town would have to wait.

"I'm sure." She patted Drake on the shoulder on the way out. He barely acknowledged her. He sat, his full attention on me.

I resisted the urge to run after her, not wanting to seem needy. I'd lived seventeen years without any knowledge of my dad. What were a few more hours?

Our conversation went fan-freakin-tastic. But only after I decided to stop feeling sorry for myself. The best thing? He didn't act all 'poor you' when I told him why I came to Adams. "My dad died when I was a baby. My mom's um…my mom and I didn't know anything about it. I just found out he died up here when he was visiting his aunt."

"So you decided to give Rose a visit?"

"Uh huh." I nodded. A little spot tugged in my stomach. Jealousy. He said her name with such familiar warmth. "How do you know her?"

"Neighbors." He shrugged. "Been neighbors for a long time. I've known her my entire life. We've become real close since my parents died. She's been like a grandma…" he trailed off, laughing a little and then set his finished drink down, swirling the glass in circles. "…or something."

I sipped at my own orange juice, washing down the French toast along with the emotions seeping in through the cracks of my pasted-on armor. I'd never had a grandma either.

"Well, Miss Miami." Drake leaned back in the chair, holding steady on two legs as he wiped his hands on a napkin. "How long are you here for?"

"Not sure. I don't know if Rose is gonna let me stay."

"She'll let you stay." He locked his hands behind his head and lifted his shoulders. "But if you want, I can have a talk with her." He paused. A cheesy Hollywood smile lit his entire face. "She loves me."

I tittered inside. This country boy charm was oddly attracting. "Thanks, but I think I'll save you for when I really need you." The little flirt line leaked out before I could stop it. When my phone vibrated in my pocket immediately after, I was glad. This was about Dad, not cute boys.

Mom texted me: **Fine. Just ignore me then. Leave me…** *And blah, blah, blah, I'm a horrible daughter.*

I pushed the Ignore button and set my cell on the table. "Here, give me your number," Drake said, taking out his phone. "You're not going to want to hang out with an old lady all the time. And…I can give you an awesome tour of the town."

His blue eyes beamed through me. If this were Miami, I might have—scratch that, would have—walked away from the country boy who said things like 'awesome tour of the town' and join friends who would already be pointing and laughing behind cupped hands. It wouldn't matter how adorable Drake was, they'd drop him and go search for a guy that looked like he walked off a GQ cover. A guy with a Ralph Lauren polo shirt and hair gel who knew how to play tennis, instead of this little boy who wore jean cargo shorts and a white Hanes t-shirt.

"Um...sure." Hell, my friends weren't here. And Mom wasn't around to give disapproving, waste-of-your-time looks. Not that that would matter. I probably would have given him my number out of spite, just never picked up if he dared call. I took his phone and handed him mine. "Give me yours too. You know, just in case I need you." There was only Rose now, and Rose seemed to adore this cute, countrified boy.

I still punched in my number when the door swung open and Rose stuck her head in. "I was thinking, why don't you give Sarah a ride around town?"

"I'm one step ahead of you, Rose," Drake said, motioning to his cell phone as I handed it back to him.

"Ugh," she sighed, "you kids and your cellular phones." Her voice traveled back to us as she walked away. "Can't you just take her now or are you too busy?" Through the swings of the door, I saw Rose's shaking head.

Drake laughed. "I thought I had to finish the lawn. Do you *want* to go now?"

"Hold on one sec." I followed after Rose into the other room and found her bent over, watering a big fern plant in the foyer. "Aunt...um, Rose? I thought maybe we could spend some time together. You know...to get to know each other?"

She set down the watering can and straightened up. "I want that too. But I'm going to be *really* busy over the next week. I didn't know you were coming and I have a bunch of commitments I need to stick to." She gave me a lopsided smile, almost like an apology. "Just go out. Have fun. Drake is a really sweet boy."

I swallowed the disappointment with my own crooked smile. "He seems it."

"Oh he is, honey. Cute, too." She stopped to wink and then continued on, "And after this week we can work on us." I nodded as the dining room door squeaked open and Drake appeared. Rose clapped her hands in front of her chest. "Great. I think Sarah's ready." She cupped my head and gave an encouraging smile before continuing to water the plant. It seemed a lot like my new aunt was setting me up. *Hmm, could be worse. He could be a dork. Or nasty looking.* "Oh," Rose called out as Drake led me to the front door. "Don't forget to give Sarah a town history lesson. Settler's Days start tonight and she'll want to know about the witches."

Chapter Two

1639

Isabella lay in a rope-strung straw mattress, a breath held in her tight chest. She listened for the stirrings of her parents who lay just beyond the brick of the fireplace in the main room. Nothing but the night sounds surrounded their timbered cottage and chirped in through the window of her tiny room.

She rose, cringing when the ropes pulled taut and groaned its displeasure at her. The rooms remained still, though, and for that she gave thanks. Isabella slipped her stockinged feet into worn leather shoes and prayed for forgiveness for her actions as of late. Her mind felt not her own.

She stepped away and moved nimbly across the planked floor before pressing her ear against the wood of the door. She held her breath. The house sat still.

She needed to be sure.

Before her, though she could scarce believe it still, was a desk made of fine wood. It was by far the most agreeable adornment that had ever graced their humble rooms. She reached to play her fingers over the wood. *Later*, she chided herself, *tomorrow I shall have a little time.*

On her new desk, a candle flickered, threatening to go out. It bent low from the draft of the window and then shot straight up again. In haste she moved forward and took a piece of parchment from her pouch. Unfolding it, Isabella leaned in toward the flame, angling the paper so she could read the familiar words written in crisp, slanted writing.

Nerves scuttled through her, like the hundreds of mice hunting the town streets. She pressed the paper against her chest and sighed. Then, careful to fold along the same edges, she closed it. Her eyes flicked towards the door, but the parchment in her hands stayed her, reminding her of still yet another chore. She must not become forgetful.

Isabella passed the door along the outside of her room, careful not to go near the center. The floorboards creaked there, even with her slight step. She made her way to the opposite corner, bent down on hands and knees, and used the nub of her finger to pry open the loose floorboard there. Once free, she grasped the board with both hands and inched it open. Isabella drew out a bundle of paper tied with sewing string. She let her eyes pause and delight a moment over the fine papers before placing the parcel on the floor next to her. Bringing the newest sacrament to her lips, she kissed it, then hid the letter with that of Thomas' others.

She replaced the board, her heart beating faster with every moment and moved to the door. Her ear rested against the wood where she heard the sounds of slumber interrupting the quiet of the night. She was now free to slink out of the house.

Without folly, Isabella slipped into the main room, making sure to avoid the areas that creaked. She spared a glance toward her parents' bed. The curtains hid their sleeping bodies. She crept further into the hall, the smell of barley still staining the air from the vegetable pottage cooked earlier, and escaped out the cottage door. Months of secret meetings allowed her to do this with little error and she soon felt the cool night air on her face.

The full moon proved enough light to see her way. Picking up her skirt, she ran across the grass, past

the hog pen, and just inside her father's barn. No
Thomas.

Out of view from the small cottage, she allowed
the fear to sweep through her. His letter implied
importance, but might this be the day Thomas did not
show? Might it be he revealed their love to the magistrate
and the magistrate forbid his son to see her again? The
feeling seized her, snapping her nerves like twigs.

Her mind so fixed in doubt, her heart gripped in
agony, she did not hear the rustling of footsteps over the
barn floor. "Good day, Isabella."

She whirled. Thomas. Suppressing a smile
bubbling like a brook inside her, she dipped and said,
"Good day." She tried to steady her breath, which came
at her now in rapid gulps. The once wash of fear turned to
relief, leaving her in a stew of mixed agitation.

"Are you well?" Concern darkened his smile and
his usual light eyes were shadowed over. His whole body
was rigid like the high masts from the great ships her
father told her of, the ones that brought him to this new
world.

"I am."

He considered her for a moment, his eyes taking
in her flushed complexion bonneted by loose blonde
strands that separated from her braid. "I am sorry I have
come later than usual. I almost did not come at all."

Isabella's heart beat like the flutter of wings. "But
your letter spoke of importance."

"I have news of the utmost importance." He
stared mute for a moment. "Another woman was taken
today. Father is so very angry and vows to let no evil pass
his notice. I do not want them to mistake…"

"I understand." A smile shadowed her face, a
secret in the dark, but she suppressed it. It was not a good

thing Thomas liked her enough to defy his father, endanger his honor, his life.

"I am tormented worrying over you. 'Tis not safe."

Isabella stepped toward him, uneasy over the turn of his face, and then paused, minding herself. It was not as if they were pledged to one another, nor did her situation in life recommend her. "My father does not speak of this to me."

"I doubt if anything should reach his ears. He is hardly ever in town, choosing to work his fields instead."

"'Tis true. My father works hard."

"He may know of Mrs. Worth though."

Isabella clenched her fists around her dress. "Mrs. Worth? I am sure it cannot be so."

"It is so. Father said."

"I doubt your father not. I am...confused. That is all."

"Everyone is not like you and I." Thomas reached for her. Untouched, his hand fell in the empty space between them. "Mrs. Worth was spotted in the woods late last night in the midst of making a fire. They found evidences of previous fires there."

"Tell me, who found her?"

"My father did not say, only revealing that Mrs. Worth has been crying out her innocence ever since." Thomas moved in, his face in earnest. "But Isabella, you know we cannot believe her. 'Tis all lies. Remember what the churchwardens have said? Listening to anything they say is blasphemous. She might trick us with a spell, do harm to us and free herself."

Isabella looked away. "I cannot believe that Mrs. Worth has signed with the devil, Thomas. She has a husband and two small children."

"Because you are too good." He took her chin in his hand and made her look in his eyes. They were light again, an intense blue that writhed her insides to knots. "You cannot fathom anyone being unlike yourself, but it is out there. This makes three now that will burn away their sins and I have not a doubt there will be more." Thomas took his eyes from hers and peered into the woods. "Their supernatural powers have kept them hidden. My father will find them out though."

Isabella bit down her trembling lip. *Surely, Mrs. Worth be a mistake.*

Determined not to waste their time together, she took a deep breath, stepped around Thomas, and leaned against the barn wall. "My father was in town today. Is that why you think he may know of Mrs. Worth?"

"I saw him. You did not think I forgot, did you?" Thomas leaned against the wall next to her. "'Tis the only reason I allowed myself to come tonight. I wanted to wish you well on your birthday."

If it were not for the darkness of the night, Thomas would see Isabella's flaming cheeks. She bit down on them, though a smile lit her face anyway. "Thank you."

"I happened to see your father carrying a rather nice gift. I asked him if he needed help, but he declined. I was hoping he would agree so that I might have seen you."

Isabella's cheeks grew a touch hotter. "I would have liked that."

His hand slowly reached for hers and she met him in the middle, palm pressing against palm. He brought her hand up by the fingers and placed a soft kiss there. "I have one request before I take my leave. Would you be so kind as to grace me with a letter written on your new desk?"

Her lips would not move. His face held all the emotion, all the devotion she had within, though she could not bring herself to voice her attachment. She turned her head to the ground and squeezed his hand.

He pressed hers in response. "I must leave." His look mirrored the loss she felt. "Farewell, dear Isabella."

"Farewell," Isabella choked out. And he was gone.

She wondered if his cheeks burned like hers, if his hand tingled at the spot where he kissed her, and if his heart thudded in his chest. It felt like a dream, a joyous dream. Only a whisper of his retreating step on the grass proved he was ever there at all.

She crept back to the house. Thomas filled her thoughts, like always. She reached her bedroom and pulled her nightclothes on, already half dreaming as she slipped into bed.

Chapter Three

Present Day

I walked through the grassy park in the middle of this unfamiliar town wondering, *What the hell did I get myself into?*

The drive around Adams earlier did not even come close to preparing me for this. Everywhere my eyes traveled, regular, seemingly normal adults, dressed in costume. Thought after sarcastic thought kept springing up. What if someone needed medical attention right now? Could a patient really let their doctor, who was dressed as a scantily clad witch with a red bra, matching G-string and thigh high boots, attend to their broken leg? Or even worse—deliver a baby? *Eww.*

Drake warned this would be weird, but this was bad. This was like Mardi Gras night at one of the clubs back home, but worse. Much worse. These people were into it. And it was everybody. The whole freakin' town was crazy.

At least not everyone wore a ho costume though, which was good, considering. Considering Adams was no Miami and there were people of all shapes and sizes in this rinky-dink town. Plenty wore the obvious, overdone witch look—faces painted green, long, thin, wart-covered noses, and pointy hats.

Oh, the hat. Now this was where the townies got clever. Black ones, purple ones, red with black lace ones and the best one yet, lime green and black striped that matched the tights the women wore. Yes, a group of them. A senior citizen group, that, from the look of their arthritic knuckles clutching straw broomsticks, probably made their way over on a bus from the local nursing home. At least they weren't the ones in the corsets and G-strings.

I can't believe my dad grew up here.

I kept it low-key. As in off the crazy radar low-key. And actually, the plain t-shirt and jeans I threw on were totally off the mark. For me, at least. The besties back in Miami wouldn't even recognize me. I could imagine Jamie pointing and laughing, making *me* the joke as they walked away with their Louis V. purses and pumps.

Hell, I didn't even recognize myself. Not in a physical way. Designer jeans or no designer jeans, I was still Sarah. The same hazel eyes, brown hair with the much-needed blonde highlights. Otherwise, I tend to look mousy. But come on, this culture earthquake I'd been riding since this morning—horrifying. Now, Rose and Drake seemed normal. Cool even. Everyone else? Not so much. I had to keep the smart-ass comments to myself earlier on the 'awesome tour of the town' so as not to offend Drake. And trust me, it was hard. Adams held so much fodder for smart-ass comments it wasn't funny.

Of course, maybe it would have been different if the first time I met them they weren't dressed in hick-town witch costumes. Maybe if they pretended to be regular people, I wouldn't have been forced to give them a nickname.

The Crazies. That's right. *The Crazies.* I was pretty partial to it.

I picked up the pace, dodging Crazies strewn out on blankets, and tried to see over stupid hats. Earlier, Drake and I arranged to meet by the concession stands, which I saw on the way into town. Getting to them was another issue. They were sandwiched in between booths, with massive amounts of people milling about. I bounced around like a pinball trying to avoid any kind of contact with a Crazy.

Finally, I broke through and spotted Drake near a hotdog stand. Well, tonight, he was Drake-the-Wizard.

"What are you wearing?" he asked as I walked up to him, a playful smile pulled at his lips.

Seriously? I should be asking him that. I peered down. "What?" I shrugged, pulling at my Abercrombie T.

"I told you to wear something witchy."

"And I told you I wouldn't be seen with you if you dressed like *that*." I pointed at his hooded black cloak.

"Rose asked me to bring you here and I refuse to let you make me look like a dork." Drake took me by the shoulders and spun me around. His breath warmed my ear in the cool evening air. "Take a look. You're the one that looks out of place."

I scanned the crowd. *Everybody* in head-to-toe costume. I was the only one who hadn't dressed up. Obviously. I was not in to looking like a moron. "It's not like it's Halloween or anything and I don't think you need help looking like a dork."

He ignored the jibe. "It's better than Halloween." Drake pushed me toward a souvenir table. "Were you not listening earlier? I told you this is about our town history, Sarah. Not some holiday where you get candy." He pointed out a black shirt with an evil witch face that read *Settler's Day Fest.*

I reached out to finger the material. I really didn't get why they wanted to celebrate their town being so hysteric over nothing. Hello. Hadn't they ever heard of Salem, Massachusetts? Innocent people died there. "Don't you think this is kind of corny?"

"No." Drake took out his wallet and handed the woman behind the table a ten. I protested, shaking my head and stepping backward, away from the cheesy witch stuff. Too late. The woman glared and threw the shirt to Drake as he tried to assure me, "So you can really get into it. It'll be more fun."

I rolled my eyes. "Listen…"

Drake tossed the shirt at my face. "Get over yourself, put the shirt on and let's go have some fun."

I scowled and tugged on the witch shirt.

He smiled a big, beautiful smile and put his arm around me. "Look. It's even glow-in-the-dark. Now that is hot."

I shoved him off and fluffed at my hair. "Whatever. I could rock a plastic bag if I wanted to."

"Yeah, a see-through one."

"He-ey." I pulled out the doe-eyed charm I'd seen my mom use countless times. Must have been a Perkins girl thing. "I thought boys from Virginia were supposed to be southern gentleman." His eyes flashed and he gripped my body tighter. *Stop. Stop. Stop. This is not why you're here.*

"I am." Drake smothered me with another smile. "I bought you the shirt, didn't I?" He grabbed for my hand. I slyly made it busy by rearranging the new shirt around myself and then slipped it into my pocket. He didn't seem to notice. "Come on. We better find a spot before the show starts."

He maneuvered through the crowd while I trailed along behind. I took short, quick steps to keep up with him and dodge other people. "Where are we going?"

"Right…here," he said, finding the perfect spot under an old oak tree. "Sit down. I'm going back to get us something to eat."

Drake swiveled around and left. The leaves of the oak blew in the wind as a pink-colored sky rolled in. Even though Adams was so last century, its beauty was tempting. *Dad must have really liked it here. It's so...different. Calm.* Miami had the ocean, beautiful sand beaches, and people. Lots and lots of people. Adams was this small dot on a map that nobody knew about except for the people living in or around it.

The town had history, however weird and creepy it may be. At least it had something. It had Dad. The only page I brought myself to read that night, while I was back at Mom's, said he was packing for a trip home to Adams. Home. A wonderful word. A word that made me think of bear hugs, of smiling faces, of kitchens that smelled like people actually cooked in them. At least, that's what I imagined it to be.

On stage, a young woman talked to two men as they set up a microphone and speakers. One of them showed her how to adjust the mic stand and the buzz of the speakers sounded as he demonstrated the on/off switch. I twisted around and searched for Drake in the crowd, finding him easily. Most of the townies sat like me now, waiting for the show, but he stood out. So did the girl he talked to.

It was the chick who waited tables at Abigail's Diner. The one who annoyingly smacked gum all the time and who Drake pointed out earlier at the busy diner as an ex-girlfriend. I probably would have figured it out all by myself considering the death glares she sent me from across the restaurant.

I didn't know how he could stand to be in her presence for even two seconds. She probably already popped her gum a gazillion times. The slut suit she wore may have helped. *Whoa. Can you say cleavage?* Her laced-too-tight red and black bodice heaved her boobage into his face.

Drake acted like a perfect gentleman though. He paid for our drinks and tried, several times, to back away.

She finally gave up when another customer stood right at the counter, tapping his dollar bill onto the metal shelf.

The lights around the park dimmed. I twisted toward the makeshift stage again. Forty feet away, a figure stood tall, elevated by the 2x4's that lay out on the grass only a few hours ago. A hooded black robe disguised the guy, not that I would know who he was anyway. The dark night, the material folding over his head, made him look like a faceless grim reaper. It was dusk and getting darker, the pink deepening to a rose red.

The robed figure lifted his hand, smooth, indifferent, a marionette being played with. His hand made a wide, sweeping horizontal arc, pointing into the faces of everybody.

My stomach twisted and turned into knots. Drake bumped into my shoulder and held out a drink as he sat down. Then, the figure yanked his hands in the air and a big blaze of fire erupted from the space between the stage and the audience. I jumped, deftly managing to spill half my soda. I barely noticed.

Flames shot up, reaching toward the night. The smell of gasoline used for ignition hung in the air. A few people laughed behind me. Drake even joined in. "Gotcha," he said, leaning over, whispering in my ear. With him so close, the cologne clinging to his long, black robe smothered the wood smoke that had filled my nostrils.

I peered at him. He turned away and pulled his hood up. He was the exact match of the person on stage.

I sat with a wizard. I talked with a wizard.

I made fun of people for things like this.

Still, I inched closer to him. The fire, the reddish sky, the grim reaper, the witches, everything. It got to me. An eerie feeling tangled itself within every thought, like something hidden watched from just beyond sight.

On the stage, the figure in the dark cloak threw back the hood. The fire glow cast the face in shadows, an ever-changing kaleidoscope of orange, red, and black. The speakers thumped, thumped, thumped as the black hooded figure tapped the front of the microphone. The hollow sound echoed throughout the open park and bounced off the surrounding buildings. No one talked. They barely even moved. Only the slight ripple of the crowd as everyone inclined their heads and inched forward, awe-struck.

The wind picked up, fueling the flames. The blazed erupted, flaring up, lighting the figure's face. I gasped.

The grim reaper wasn't a guy. It was Rose.

Drake peeked over at me, his eyebrows knit together. "You okay?"

"That's my aunt," I whispered loud, still trying to comprehend it myself. "What is she doing up there?"

"She's the leader."

"Huh?" Uneasiness squeezed my chest, like the time I went to see that stupid Ouija board movie with friends. They all laughed through the scary parts while I spent most of the movie with my heart trembling and one second away from closing my eyes. "Leader of what?"

"This." Drake opened his arms wide and twisted his body, scanning the corners of the five-sided park. "She puts all this together."

I took it all in. Giant banners announced "Adams Colonization", eerie witch posters and mannequins with stringy green hair and large, red eyeballs stared back. The guards along the stage dressed in old brown suits and hats I guessed were supposed to be replicas of what the first settlers wore. The costumes reminded me of pilgrims. They stood at attention, faces impassible as they monitored the crowd. The picture sank into my brain, this parallel reality where past met present in a jumbled mesh.

Drake leaned into me again. "Sorry. I should have told you."

No wonder why she said she was too busy to hang out with me. I snuck forward a little, caught up in the surprise appearance of Rose. The arm that had been touching Drake instantly chilled. He was so nice. And cute. But the reason why I came here was up on that stage.

Rose's voice rang out, low and seductive. "On this day in 1610, our ancestors inhabited a foreign land. Today, we call that piece of land Adams, Virginia." Scattered applause swelled through the park. "Our ancestors brought with them superstition…and fear from England. Men and women, children—all terrified of one thing." Rose's hypnotic voice was mesmerizing and I leaned forward even more. "Witches." The stare of an old, wise woman lingered over everybody and when her eyes met mine, a pool of black reflected the licking orange flames.

"They fled here, terrified of the supernatural. They hoped to start a new life. One without the constant paranoia. They failed. Our ancestors lived in complete, maddening, unrelenting fear their entire lives. Are we like them?" Audible no's and descending grunts rose from the crowd. "No. We're not." Her voice pitched higher, and louder. "Today, we embrace our history. Today, we stare the supernatural in the face and laugh at it." Loud cheers erupted from every corner of the park and Rose shouted over them, "Today, we celebrate!"

Rose motioned to the side of the reaching flames. Two men in the ugly brown trousers and jackets nodded. "During this opening ceremony, we will conquer fear as they did back in the old days." The men pulled at ropes, hoisting a cross into the air. Mounted to the cross beam was the body of a woman, her mouth agape in horror.

I drew in a sharp breath. I felt Drake move next to me so I turned my gaze on him. A sly smile graced his face. He put his arm around me, pulling me closer. "Are you scared?" he whispered.

I couldn't speak. These people *were* freakin' crazy. My eyes darted through the crowd, looking for a policeman—somebody—who might stop this.

"Don't worry. We always do this on opening night," Drake said, pulling me even closer, rubbing my shoulder with his hand.

I wanted to scream at him to do something, to help the poor woman. He only sat smiling, eyes bright with anticipation. I knocked his hand off me and pulled away, but before I could wiggle free of Drake's arms and run to the fire pit, the cotton clothes the woman wore caught fire from the reaching flames underneath. My breath clogged my throat. I didn't know whether to scream first, or cry.

The flames spread fast. The waistline already edged with black char before the fire incinerated it. Dark gray smoke furled over the helpless woman and puffed up toward the blood red sky.

ERIN BUTLER

Chapter Four

1639

Isabella stared at the timbered ceiling, a chill freezing her to her core. When sleep had come to her earlier, it threw her in fits of nightmares, soaking her bedclothes through with sweat. The damp linen cloaked her in cold terror.

For hours, as surely the sun would be forging daybreak by now, sick images threatened beyond mindfulness, beyond waking truths. A line of women on wooden crosses drifted past her eyes. Dark red and orange flames enveloped the screaming, crying women, as one after the other, a bed of hay and blackthorn at their feet caught fire from Magistrate Ludington's torch.

She saw Mrs. Worth, her two children reaching out for her. Louisa Pyle gone mad, pleading with her parents to save her. Martha Compton was trying to break free, the cross swaying to and fro until the first lick of flames got her.

Then there were two on the end, who she recognized not, for their faces turned in toward one another. They did not weep or struggle, but stood proud, unfeigned, until a gentleman from the swarming crowd of villagers came forth from the shadows.

Father?

It was him. She could do nothing but watch as he paled white with the anger filling him. There was a set to his shoulders, a stiffness settling in that she recognized from the evenings when he had done all he could in the fields with little to show for it. The two women turned toward him, revealing their faces.

They had the same golden yellow hair, made brighter by the fire now burning at their feet. The same color hair Isabella could feel now, matted to her neck in the sanctity of her bed. The same color hair Thomas called 'the hair of angels'.

Orange flames reflected off single tears that sparkled like stars, two tears that dripped from the faces of her and her mother. Tears shed for their husband, for their father, who must now live without them.

Isabella found it impossible to keep the images from her mind though her eyes were dry and tired from staring relentlessly upwards to see every corner of the dark room and the jumping shadows that hid there.

Mrs. Worth? Impossible. She manages a family, a husband, which she honors and respects.

Isabella drew in a fearful breath. Her head ached from lack of sleep. Though Thomas would call her naïve, a country girl, she believed Mrs. Worth to be a righteous woman. As righteous as her or her mother.

Isabella tore the covers from her and moved to the desk her father purchased for her birthday. Just enough moonlight leaked in through the window to write and she wanted a letter for Thomas as he asked. She dared not use up another candle for Mrs. Lynne would scold her again.

Isabella trailed her fingers along the wood and then around the outside. They brushed along a row of ridges. She twisted to see what her fingers found. There, in the very corner of the small desk was an S dug into the wood. Isabella's breath caught in her throat.

S? Shipton? She held her hands to her chest.

The bedroom door swung open, crashing against the other wall. Isabella jumped. Her mother stood there, face blanched white and eyes wide. "Moth—?"

Mrs. Lynne brought a finger to her lips. "Make a sound not." Her mother's hair fell loose and wild around her. Isabella heeded her warning. She made no other move and barely even a breath came to her.

Three faint knocks sounded from within. "Come." Her mother seized her hand, pulling her upright and straight through to the front entry.

Her father crouched down in shadows, peeking through the window. "Go," he demanded, his voice an urgent whisper.

Mrs. Lynne's hold clamped tighter around her daughter's hand and soon, a blast of cool air whipped at their faces as they ran from the house. Isabella's heart stuttered and skipped furiously as her bare feet slipped over the wet grass. Her soles stung as they scraped along stones and broken branches.

Her mother's eyes darted from the road to the woods and back again. Isabella ran along beside her, the damp night air prickling her skin. The barn loomed ahead, darker than the moon tinged sky around it. Mrs. Lynne barreled through the shadowy entrance and led Isabella to a back corner where an old blanket lay. "Stay."

Isabella watched Mrs. Lynne escape into the recesses of the barn. Blackness greeted her everywhere. Only shafts of moonlight from the spaces in the wood gave her reprieve from the dark. Her breath came in gasps, the cold air stinging her throat. She knelt down on the blanket and tried to see out the cracks, but found the gap not wide enough for her eye.

A soft hand touched her back. She started, and clamored around, her heels tugging against the blanket. Again with a finger to her lips, Mrs. Lynne stood over her and thrust a blanket in her lap. Isabella enveloped herself in it.

Men's voices sounded from the road. Isabella gasped before her mother's hand covered her mouth.

Thomas.

His voice mingled among others. "Are you certain, Father?" she heard him ask.

Her heart pounded in her head, drowning out the response. Mrs. Lynne knelt next to her on the blanket and hugged her tight. Placing her lips near her daughter's ear, she whispered, "Do not say a word. I believe they are not coming for us, but we do not want to reveal our hiding place."

Isabella nodded, not trusting words to come out inaudible. She feared if she tried to speak at all, a cry might fall from her lips. Then they would be ruined.

The voices passed and every second made Isabella relax a little more. Questions threatened to stream from her mouth. Minutes came and left, and only the sounds of the forest carried on the wind.

Footsteps sounded in the barn and Mrs. Lynne raised herself up.

Isabella shuddered. Her father's fists were clenched for a fight and his features were drawn together in fury. "They have gone."

"Edward," her mother cried, reaching for him.

His face softened. "My wife," he said, gathering her in his arms. "We are safe for now." Mr. Lynne motioned for Isabella to get up. "My beautiful women," he said and kissed them both on the foreheads before holding them in a long embrace. Mrs. Lynne's shoulders shook with emotion. "Let us go back to the house."

He hastened them through the night and back into the dark house to Isabella's room.

She broke free and faced her father. "What is happening? You must tell me."

"I am sorry I have tried to keep it from you." Mr. Lynne looked away and sighed. "There was once a time when we lived only in fear of the savages of this new land. At present, we must worry over the very men we sit in the meetinghouse with." He turned back, eyes wide. "Daughter, Mrs. Worth was burned this night as a witch."

Isabella grasped for her father's hand. "Burned?"

He smoothed her hair down and caught her by the shoulders. "I do not believe Mrs. Worth be a witch. Magistrate Ludington errs in his judgment." He began walking the tiny room. "What am I to do?" he asked, staring at the walls. Mrs. Lynne's shoulders heaved still and she let out a sob. Mr. Lynne moved toward them. "I must only think of our family." He pushed them down on the bed.

"And the men?" Isabella asked.

"A witch-hunting party."

"And what is their intention?"

"They search for signs of the devil, Child. We cannot be too careful."

Mrs. Lynne wiped at her eyes with the seam of her nightshirt. Her husband knelt beside them, a hand aside either one on the hand-sewn blanket. Mrs. Lynne patted Isabella's leg and then promised, "We will do what you wish."

Mr. Lynne nodded. "If this should ever happen again, Isabella, do as your mother says. I have given her instructions that you need not worry yourself over now. If the time comes, you do what she tells you. Understand?"

"If the time comes? I know not—"

"If they come for us."

Isabella's hand flew to her mouth. "But we are not Satan's witches."

"Of course not," her father spat the words. "I believe strongly that Mrs. Worth was otherwise too when she was taken."

Isabella's heart drummed loud in her ears. "And you think this might happen to us?"

"To anyone."

Tears streamed down Isabella's cheeks. Mr. Lynne cursed and strode from the room, the boards creaking underneath his heavy step.

Isabella drew in a long breath, lost inside herself. "I heard one of them say something."

The bed groaned as her mother stood. Isabella looked to her, forgetting she was even there. "I did as well," Mrs. Lynne said.

"What do you think they looked for?"

"I imagine for anything suspicious."

"What about Mrs. Worth?"

"I cannot care about that now." Her mother grabbed up her hand and squeezed it. "I want only to protect us."

"And Mrs. Shipton?"

Mrs. Lynne cocked her head. "What of her? She has not been taken."

Isabella looked over at the desk, at the mark of the S burnt onto it and shuddered. "Do you think she will?"

Chapter Five

Present Day

The bed was my friend.

I awoke, sprawled spread eagle across every inch of the queen-size mattress. Light shone through the windows making it seem like full day outside, but I had a sinking suspicion it was early. Too early.

Over 400 years of history. They weren't kidding. It was a long, long night. My head throbbed, reminding me I stayed up way too late. The lingering smell of gasoline and the raucous crowd still echoed between my ears.

Sleep still clouding my eyes, I searched the room for the clock on the desk. I forgot to pull tight the curtains last night, allowing the sun to seep in super early and then get really annoying at about, oh… right now. 8:09 exactly, the digital clock blinking red informed me.

Note to self: Pull your curtains shut from now on. No more of this waking up early crap.

I sat up and stretched. The black witch shirt still clung to me. The only strength I could muster last night was unfastening my bra before collapsing on the bed, already half-asleep before hitting the flowery comforter.

My phone buzzed on the nightstand. Okay. And I had time to take the phone out of my pocket. But that was a necessity.

It was a text from Jamie. *Great. Utterly Fantastic.*

saw ur mom yesterday seems upset

Yeah right. Friends at home still weren't used to my mother's drama induced, poor-me-I'm-so-abused BS. *Ignore.*

My phone buzzed again. *Seriously?*

Mom. "Ugh. What now?"

Thought u were gonna call me yesterday???????? I hope u r on ur way home!!!!!!

The phone vibrated in my hands again. "Oh my god," I screamed into the pillow. "It's too early for this crap."

Drake. *Thank god.*

Mornin' Sunshine. U and me. Breakfast.

A grin widened across my face. It buzzed again.

Abigail's 9:30!

K, I texted back.

I readied myself in a hurry and ran downstairs, wanting to tell Rose I wouldn't be needing the uber deluxe breakfast treatment this morning. "Rose?" I called into the kitchen. No answer. I hadn't seen her since last night at the ceremony. I even got home before she did. Talk about lame.

She wasn't joking about being busy this week. Uneasiness swept over me. Not because Rose wouldn't be around to talk about my dad, but because I didn't want to seem like a nuisance. I had come at a bad time.

"Rose?" I called again, in the foyer now. *What? Had she stayed out all night?*

I pushed open a door to the left of the dining room that I hadn't been in yet. The room was bright with natural light from one wall full of windows overlooking the backyard garden. A fireplace nestled in the corner on the opposite side.

A library.

A long cream-colored couch faced the fireplace, and matching armchairs at the ends of the room faced the windows. Bookshelves brimming with books lined the walls. Most were leather-bound and the titles on the spine were barely legible, gold text flaking off.

A real library. An actual in-house library. I thought royalty and rich people were the only ones who thought to include libraries. Or the only ones who could afford to act like they actually used a house library.

I grinned and walked to the closest bookshelf, trailing my finger over the spines before picking one at random. My breath caught. "What the heck?" I frowned, my finger tracing the word 'Journal' on the cover.

A sharp rap on the door startled me and I dropped the book. It thudded on the carpeted floor. "What are you doing in here?"

I turned. It was only Rose. I laughed, the initial jolt of nerves toning down a notch. "I was looking for you. Drake asked me to meet him for breakfast, so…" I stopped short. Rose glared down at the book on the floor beside my feet. "Um, sorry about that. You scared me and I dropped it."

"You are not allowed in here."

"What?" I asked, but an icy stare from Rose silenced me. "I mean, yeah, sure, but…" I bent over and picked up the journal. "…this looks exactly like the journal I found of my father's."

Rose's eyebrows drew together as she walked up to me, tearing the leather book from my hands. "You are not allowed in here." She put the book back in its place and pointed toward the door.

My face flushed. "I'm sorry, Rose. I was looking for you and saw that journal. It looks just like my father's. Are they *all* his in here?"

"No," Rose shot back as I stepped out into the foyer, her hostility pushing me from behind. "Those aren't David's." She stopped in the doorway, arms crossed.

Great. I've pissed her off. "I enjoyed the…" A pause left the air between us buzzing. I searched for an appropriate sounding word. "…festivities last night."

"Good."

Okay. Still pissed. What else can I talk about? I pulled the hem of my shirt down, fingers grazing against the cell phone in my pocket. "Hey, did you call my mom again yesterday? Because she texted me this morning and—"

"No, I didn't. I was busy getting ready for the festival." She hadn't moved her imposing figure an inch from the library doorway.

"Yeah, I understand. I just…" *needed something else to say.* I reached up to play with the collar of my crew neck shirt.

"I'll take care of it, Sarah." Her voice rang with the stern confidence of a drill sergeant. She reached behind her and pulled the door shut. "Tell Drake I say hello."

****

I ran a hand through my hair as I walked into Abigail's. My heart hummed with guilt. *Leave it to me to get in an argument with my aunt already. It hasn't even been forty-eight hours.* Seeing Drake put me at ease a little though and seeing Drake in his present situation made me giggle.

He sat at the counter and pretended to read the paper, deflecting the gum-smacking bimbo's—aka his ex, aka the reason why I quickly curled my hair this morning—attempts at conversation. She hovered around him, pretending to wipe down counters and fill salt and pepper shakers, sneaking glances to see if he needed anything. You had to give her credit. She tried.

"Hey," I said, sitting down on the stool next to his.

"You're late." He widened his eyes to convey the torture he endured.

"Sorry." I couldn't hold it in anymore so I half-giggled, half-asked the next question. "What's on the agenda for today?"

"Food." His face was solemn, serious and his tone was matter-of-fact.

"Food?"

"Yes. Definitely food." He folded the paper and placed it on the counter. Marlene came right over and straightened it in front of him. Her arms stretched the entire length of the counter as she tapped the inner sections back in line, her hands lingering. Drake ignored her and kept talking. "Then…they're having a bunch of cool things going on around town. We can watch a mock witch trial." His voice became lighter. "Explore the first settlers, attend a real Wiccan meeting…. Well, you get the gist. We can pretty much do whatever, whenever." He paused to take a sip from his drink. Hovering Marlene took the opportunity to wipe the white-speckled Formica in front of him. *Is this girl serious?* "They have the same type of things going on all week. So, whatever you want to do is fine with me."

I smiled at the waitress before shaking out my hair and then placed a runaway curl around my ear. *Thank you. You can leave now*, was what I wanted to say. She waited nearby like a hungry, homeless puppy.

I turned to Drake. The incident this morning in the library left me gnawing for more information about Dad. Maybe he could help me find out what kind of person he was, since Rose was too busy. "What do you think…" I glanced at Marlene who didn't even try to hide the fact she was eavesdropping on us, and lowered my voice. "What do you think my dad would have done?"

The question piqued the all-too-eager table busser's interest. "Your dad?"

"Oh, that's right." Drake gestured with one hand like he had totally forgotten to introduce us and with the other, he squeezed my thigh underneath the counter. "Marlene, you haven't met Sarah yet. Sarah, Marlene, Marlene Sarah." To Marlene, he said, "Her dad used to live here."

"Well, why didn't *he* bring you here?" Marlene asked, her eyes rolling in the back of her dumb head.

"Well," I mimicked her. No one was a better eye roller than me. "He's actually really busy being dead, so…"

"What about your mom?" Marlene interrupted. Some people might have felt bad and just. Stopped. Talking. Not Marlene. "Wouldn't she be the best one to tell you about your dad? You didn't have to come all this way." *Not-too-subtle hint. Point taken.*

Drake opened his mouth, but I started talking first. "She's actually really busy being a bitch. So, no." I put my hand on his shoulder. "I just have Drake." He leaned back and crossed his arms, a smile twisting the corners of his mouth. He seemed to be enjoying this.

"Well, then," Marlene said, defeated for the moment, "you're definitely lucky to have found him. He just loves this stuff." She smiled wide, her face overexcited, like she was seeing Disney World for the first time. She reached over and started to rub Drake's hand.

I took mine away from his shoulder. No way was I going to get into a territorial boy fight with this backcountry skankarella. I picked up the *Adams Gazette* and ignored them.

"I think I'm the lucky one," Drake said. He pulled his hand away and placed it in his lap. He smiled at me out of the corner of his mouth. Then, he turned back to Marlene. "Anyway…how about you get us some menus so we can order?"

Marlene's feet stayed cemented on the other side of the counter. "Where are you staying?"

I completely ignored her until Drake nudged my chair with his foot. "With my aunt." I sighed, pretending to be bored.

"And that would be…?"

I let the paper drop to the counter with a splat. All the insides Marlene had straightened up so nicely earlier, spilled out on the white Formica. Then, turning a huge smile toward the stupid, foolish, ignorant, backwoods, Crazy, I started to say, "Rose McCal—"

"Rose McCallister?" Marlene's face paled and she laughed, smacking the counter. "Of course. That's a great fit, isn't it?"

"Excuse me?" Heat rushed through my body.

"Marlene," Drake said, his voice taking on a warning tone.

She ignored him. "She's a witch." Marlene's eyebrows popped. She leaned over the counter and whispered, "Didn't Drake tell you?"

"Tell me what?" I let the hint of a smile linger on my face, even though the rest of my body went rigid. What the heck did this girl know about my family that I didn't? Rose, a witch? Please. Was this girl on drugs?

"Knock it off, Marlene." Drake's voice came out gruff, making me stiffen even more on the stool. "Just get us some menus."

She pulled out a pen and pad from her apron and started to write, like she hadn't said anything at all. "Don't you want the *ushe*?"

"Sarah needs a menu." He over-pronounced my name like he was talking to a foreigner who couldn't understand English.

Marlene walked away, swaying her butt back and forth, which meant his not-too-subtle hint didn't faze her.

"What the hell was that all about?" I whispered.

"Don't worry about it." He took another sip from the mug, drawing it out this time, ending the conversation.

"That's not likely."

****

"So, here we are," Drake said, pointing down Main Street toward downtown Adams. *Downtown? His word. Not mine.* We had walked the few blocks from Abigail's after we shoveled food into our mouths, trying to get away from the prying Marlene.

Downtown consisted of one long street. It was small. All the businesses hooked together and were made out of the same red brick. Some of the buildings were taller than others and the only distinguishing thing about them were the windows and the signs above the doorways announcing what they were.

I felt like I was on an old movie set and expected to see horses and carriages, with people wearing top hats and girls barely breathing because of their restricting corsets.

The parking spaces all angled in toward the center of a long grassy area lined with benches, pink and purple flowering shrubs, and right in the middle, a statue of the first settler. I squinted to read the name. The only letter I could make out was a C.

It all seemed too quaint to me, like an illusion that could be easily wiped away, showing the hard reality underneath. I was used to living in gated communities and cities with more than one stoplight, places people around here probably only dreamt about. I had to admit, though, this was nice. The houses and businesses were immaculate. Everything was clean in an old-fashioned way. I imagined my dad happy growing up here. He called Adams home. Home. An alien planet I had yet to discover.

Drake led me down the sidewalk, past the big, black-iron lampposts and signs stating "Special Settler's Day Sales" in the little trinket shops' windows. We turned toward the park where the opening ceremony took place last night.

Today, the park attracted just as many Crazies. Carnival-like games, bounce houses and slides, concession stands, and booths littered the grounds. Signs announced "Marla the Magnificent" and "Psychic Sam".

At Abigail's, Drake saw the advertisement for the Psychic Fair in the *Adams Gazette* and pointed it out. "You want to know what your dad would have done? This is it," he said, tapping the paper on a black and white crystal ball that took up half the page.

So here we were, making our way there. Drake stopped us, eyes shining. He grabbed me by the wrist and tugged me toward a table with a sign that read "Palm Readings $5 by Jennie". *At least Jennie doesn't sound like a psychic's name. Hopefully she won't be a lunatic.*

Drake and I sat down in front of the rather normal looking girl who was barely older than me. She was probably Drake's age and appeared to be sane, like someone you might come across in a grocery store, green polo shirt and jeans with shoulder-length blonde hair. "Hello," she said. "I'm Jennie."

I smiled back at her and went to say hi, but Drake launched right in. "Sarah here needs her palm read."

My mouth dropped, unsure. "Really?" I assumed *he* would be the one getting the reading. Besides, I didn't believe, or like, all the hocus-pocus, "see into your future" crap.

"Definitely," he answered.

Psychic Jennie held her hand out, waiting for mine. I hesitated, peeked down at the fingers clutching my thighs and shrugged. What could this girl tell me that I didn't already know? Finally, palm up, I placed my right hand in Jennie's.

I flinched at her icy skin. "Sorry. For some reason, my hands are always freezing." Jennie picked up my hand and bent over it. "Any particular question you have?" she asked, still staring at my palm, moving it up and down and side-to-side to get a better view.

"Well, I…um…"

"You're not into this are you?" The palm reader looked up at me, her lips a thin line.

Wow, you're good. "No. Not really," I admitted.

"I can tell." Jennie tilted my palm and pointed at a creased line. "Right here." She tapped the line. "I can tell." Jennie's tone was mocking and her eyes darkened.

My face grew hot. *Such a stupid idea.* "This wasn't my—"

"But listen," Jennie started again, "sometime, you might need something to believe in. And when the time comes, you should believe in it."

I stared at her, blinking. *Okay. Maybe not so normal, a Crazy it is then.*

"Nice," Drake said. "You got a spooky one." He made creepy "oooh" sounds until I stopped giving the freaky girl a death stare. He pulled out his wallet to hand Jennie a five-dollar bill.

The psychic stopped him, face muted sober. "I'll do you both for five, okay?"

"Yes." I broke into a huge smile and nodded, grabbing Drake's hand and forcing it across the table. If I got a crazy reading, so would he.

Jennie did the same to him, twisting and turning his palm, trying to find the lines she needed. "Do *you* have a specific question?"

"Hmmm. Let me think." He drummed his fingers against his chin. "What does my love life look like?"

Jennie smirked, eyes peeking to me. She brought his hand closer to her face, staring at it awhile before her eyes fluttered close. Her chest rose and fell with a seriously big breath. She repeated that a few times before I nudged Drake's leg and choked back a giggle. He shifted his gaze to me with an 'Is this girl crazy?' face.

Jennie's eyes popped open. We both snapped back to attention, like we were scared of getting caught slipping notes back and forth in health class. "Your lines are much like hers." She motioned with his palm toward me. "The heart line is deep and crisp and starts below your index finger, meaning you'll be content. See the way it curves upwards?" Jennie asked, tracing her finger along Drake's line. "That means you're a romantic." She smiled at me with no emotion. "The intersecting lines here, which look like an asterisk? Palm readers call that a star. A star along the heart line means you'll have a happy marriage. You also have another fainter line here. It kind of mirrors your true heart line, runs parallel with it. That means your loved one will always protect you."

"Thank you," Drake said, eyes glassy and with an even voice lacking any of the earlier humor. When we got up and walked away, he said, "Whew. I was hoping she wouldn't bring up all my other girlfriends." He winked at me and I nudged him with my shoulder, a bogus, shocked look on my face. He took my hand and led me through the crowd. "So, you liked it?" he asked.

"Yeah, I guess so. For entertainment purposes only."

"Good. I was worried you'd think it was stupid."

"I do kinda. I'm glad you didn't take me to anyone like that." I pointed out a psychic who happened to resemble a gypsy. The woman's onyx-black poodle hair and flashy cloth headband attracted a lot of attention with the Crazies. At least twenty people stood in line.

"There's Rose," Drake observed, arcing his chin to a spot behind the popular psychic. She leaned over the woman and whispered in her ear.

"Huh. I wonder what she's saying to her."

"She's probably telling her to get a move on." Drake called out and waved, "Hi, Rose."

Rose's eyes lit up when she saw him and waved back.

Still conscious of the semi-fight we had earlier, I didn't do or say anything, only smiled a little. "What's wrong with you?" Drake asked, pulling me to a stop. "Your aunt waved over here and you didn't wave back."

I sighed. "We got in a little bit of a fight earlier. I guess."

Drake laughed. "A fight? About what?"

"She found me in the library and told me I couldn't go in there."

"Well, it is *her* house."

"No kidding." His face was open, caring, with soft lines highlighting his features. But his chin was rigid, firmly set. I wanted him to understand. "I found a journal in there that looks just like my dad's. She shooed me out and told me there wasn't anything of my dad's in there."

"Probably because there's not." He dropped my hand.

"Just…fine," I sputtered. "Excuse me for wanting to know." I crossed my arms in front of my chest.

"Sarah," Drake sighed my name like I was being stupid. "I know why she wants you to stay out of there." He reached up and moved my hair off my shoulders, even played with one of the curls. "A lot of the old books are kept in her library. She has old journals and things from the first settlers." He paused and unwound my hands from my body. "You probably freaked her out when you went in there and it shocked her. Did you give her a chance to explain? She's not used to living with someone, you know?"

"Yeah, I know."

Drake's attention flicked toward Rose again. "My dad even told me once that she has a lot of books about Wicca in there." His voice faded to a whisper.

"What?" My mouth dropped and my hand reflexively tightened around his. "Is she a witch? I mean, is she really a witch, Drake, like Marlene said?"

"No." His eyes flashed. "She was doing research to tie the old journals into modern and ancient practices. To find out if some of the villagers back in the day were actually witches. That's probably where the rumors got started."

"Did she find anything?"

"I don't know. My parents died before I could ask about it again." Drake's eyes shifted and he stared off at nothing. "Actually, I haven't thought about that since the accident."

I put my arms around him before I even realized I moved. It was reflexive, like catching a falling baby or breathing in the perfumed smell of flowers.

He smiled down at me, eyes creasing at the corners. There was a different hesitation to him. Not like he was uncomfortable, but like he thought any sudden movement might scare me away. "Thanks." I watched his lips part and fall back into place. They looked smooth, like unworn silk. "Sooo…," he said, obviously trying to change the subject. A light touch trailed down my spine, sending my heart thumping. I wanted to kiss him in the worst way. To feel the soft touch of him on my lips, his muscled body embracing me. "Do you want to do anything else? Psychic readings, crystal balls, tea leaves, anything?"

Oh, I could think of a few things. None of them involved other people, though. "I don't know." I hesitated. "The rest of these people seem kinda out there."

Drake's eyes scanned the crowd and I followed his gaze, looking for a normal psychic. Realizing that that in and of itself was ironic, I gave up.

Instead, I stood watching townies wait in long lines and shell out five dollars here and ten dollars there to learn things they already should know about themselves. Both the men and the women observed their psychics with bated breath as they performed their little rituals and made lavish predictions.

I even saw a man leave one psychic just to wait in line for another, clutching a picture between his fingers. I stepped away from Drake's grasp and watched as the man stared down at the photo. My heart hurt for him. Was it his wife? His kid? Mom or dad?

Dad.

What was I doing finding a guy when I needed to be learning about my dad? I wanted to do things my dad would have done, and I doubt he would have enjoyed the touch of Drake's hands on his back. What was wrong with me?

Drake turned. "Hey. Do you mind if I go and say hi to Pete over there? I haven't talked to him in a while." I followed his eyes. They landed on who I presumed to be Pete, a guy about Drake's age with dark brown hair. He stood at a booth motioning for him to come over, drinking from a water bottle and flirting it up with a young psychic.

"'Course not."

Drake smiled and jogged over. I heard him call "Hey" before I turned and walked amongst the Crazies all by myself. I surveyed the crowd and noticed people hadn't dressed up like they had yesterday. Adams almost seemed normal. Quaint, but normal.

A cold hand gripped my wrist. I jumped and whirled, expecting Drake. Instead, I stared into Jennie's face, dark and intense. I matched hers. "What the hell?"

"You've got to come with me." The veins in Jennie's forehead bulged as she tried to drag me behind a booth.

I tugged back, wrist burning, skin twisting. "What is your problem?" I leered at the palm reader's hold in disbelief. "You need to let me go."

"And you need to listen to me."

I stopped trying to dislodge my wrist from Jennie's grasp. "Then you need to talk faster." I didn't really have any other option. Jennie was a freak, yes. Weak? No.

"You are in danger. I didn't want to say anything in front of your boyfriend, but he...he's no good," she blurted, her whispered voice rising.

My first thought was to yell, *He's not my boyfriend. God.* Instead, I rolled my eyes. "What are you talking about?"

"I saw it. He's filled with anger...and evil..."

I laughed. Maybe not the best thing to do when a weirdo has a death grip on you, but I couldn't contain it. "So you don't even know Drake?"

"No." The psychic's voice turned haughty.

"Well, if that's all you got to go on, I'm glad I don't believe in all this voodoo stuff."

"I know what I saw."

"Sure," I said. Jennie's grasp loosened so I tugged my hand free.

"He'll hurt you." I gave one last glance at the palm reader, remembering how just a short time ago I thought she was normal and turned to walk away. A soft voice sounded from behind. "You'll end up like your dad." I stopped and slowly turned. "I didn't give you the full reading before." Her haunted eyes sent pings of dread through me, like the tense moments before Mom came striding in with a new 'guy friend' and I'd go hide in the bathroom with the shower on and cry. "Your dad died here, right?"

"Y-yes. He had a heart attack."

Jennie laughed. The vicious sound echoed in my head. "He didn't have a heart attack. He was killed."

"What?" I asked. The earth rolled underneath me, shaking everything solid and concrete and turning it to tatters.

Jennie's eyes darted around me, voice coming out in a hoarse whisper, "You'll see, Sarah. You'll see."

Someone called out, "Hey…Sarah…" I peeked back and spotted Drake walking toward us. "Is everything okay?"

I faced front again. Jennie left. Gone. "Yeah," I huffed. "Tell me. Are you the only sane one in this town?"

"Okay, spill. I saw you talking to that palm reader and it didn't look cheery." He came right up to me, looking around, eyes scanning the crowd, like my own personal secret service. "What did she want? More money for the reading?"

"No. She was giving me one I didn't ask for."

Chapter Six

1639

Threads of fog weaved their way in and out of the dense trees. The cold, brittle branches snapped as Isabella walked into the forest. The rays of the moon barely reached the earthen floor, the high canopy of trees forbid the light.

Isabella shivered, but still she marched on. Her feet stepping one after another, searching for what her mind knew not of. She drew her nightshirt closer to her, swathing herself in its warmth. From deep within the shadows, a light grew, reaching out to Isabella, beckoning her. Her pace quickened, body racking with cold tremors. Light meant heat and heat she needed.

A singsong voice floated along the fog to her, enveloping her in its melody. She was not alone. Another traveler sought out the heat in this damp night. She trudged on, not moving the chaos of branches that scratched at her face, wanting nothing more than to search out the light.

The forest broke into a clearing. A small fire sent shadows jumping into the thicket of trees, reaching farther out into the dark. Breathless and shaking, Isabella stepped into the light. The heat of the flames warmed her in an instant.

A woman stood across the clearing, her back to Isabella and the fire. Her hands stretched high above and her voice still sang the beautiful melody. Isabella stepped forward, needing to thank the woman for the use of the fire.

The woman's head cocked to the side, a small smile played against her lips. "I see you," the woman said. Isabella stumbled backwards as the woman turned, the blaze flickering on her face.

Mrs. Shipton.

Isabella awoke with a jolt. She sat straight up in bed, her chest heaving fast and her aching, tightly stretched muscles begged for release. Her blonde hair so damp it clung to her neck and face. Isabella's gaze darted around the cold, black room. Searching. Fog clouded her vision, disturbing her, but she finally locked on her target. The desk.

It glowed crimson in the early morning light that reflected off the window.

The door to her bedroom burst open. Her mother stood in the entryway, gasping for air, her hair wild and eyes wide like before.

Isabella clenched her bed sheets, tangling them in her fists and bringing them tight around her neck. It was time.

Tears streamed down her face. She knew she needed to be silent, yet they kept coming as sobs broke her chest. "Dear Isabella, are you well?"

"They have come."

"Who has come? I heard your screams."

"You are here because they have come to take me."

Mrs. Lynne flew to the bedside and gathered Isabella in a hug. "Oh no, Child. I came because you were screaming. Are you well?"

Isabella lifted her head to the desk. It did not glow. Mrs. Shipton was not before her. "I must have had a nightmare," she breathed, her cries quieting.

"The screams were terrible. I thought you were inflicted." Her mother hugged her tighter to her, sinking that word through her skin and into her insides so fast that Isabella wanted to choke on it. *Inflicted.* On Sundays, the fearful word was hammered into her by the Reverend Samuel Ludington at the meetinghouse. It meant horrible, tortured, unfathomable things. "But of course you are having nightmares," her mother continued. "We are living in the devil's hell. One cannot tell whether we are awake or if sleep has taken us." Her mother looked deep into her eyes. "And of what were you dreaming?"

"I do not remember, but I assure you I am well." Isabella tried to smile. She did not know what she saw or the reality of it. *One cannot tell whether we are awake of if sleep has taken us.* But she knew of infliction and of the images that conjured.

Mrs. Lynne's eyes grew lighter and she sighed, smoothing Isabella's hair from her face. "Oh, my dear, you scratched yourself." Isabella's heart thundered inside. She barely felt anything as her mother took the blanket from the bed and wiped at her face. She was in her nightmare, running through thickets of trees, running through needle-like branches. "Dream sweet dreams," Mrs. Lynne chastised. Then her mother was gone with the wooden door shut behind her.

Isabella lay back down in bed. Her eyes wide open, whipping back and forth about the room again. Too scared to shut them. Too scared to be thought of as inflicted. Too scared to see again what she already saw. Mrs. Shipton in the woods outside her house. There is a clearing to the north, for surely Isabella had passed it many times. Though never before had she seen Mrs. Shipton with eyes that glowed like fire.

ERIN BUTLER

Chapter Seven

Present Day

Blaming parents for things was easy. Blaming parents for everything was easy, actually.

An excellent memory, I could remember things back to when I was four. I could recall the only and exact time my mom and I ever discussed Dad being dead.

I sat at a desk in my pre-K class at Elm Street Elementary, head propped up, fingers tracing lines my pencil had made all day. The eraser-left-behinds were all piled up neatly in the pencil catch at the top of the tan desk.

I pushed some off the edge of the desk and peered over, watching them collect on the floor. Nothing. I bore a hole into my mother's back. Still talking to Miss Marty. Not even a glance my way. So, I pushed another pile right near the edge and looked up again. Mom made wide circles with her hands and laughed that big, annoying laugh.

I pushed the pile off. Nothing again. I made yet another pile of red squiggles and held my finger at the ready. Miss Marty laughed this time. My mother only smirked. It was the 'I don't really care to pay attention' smile I'd become used to. The one I found when showing Mom that I caught a butterfly with the net they gave me at school. Or the one I found when I showed my mom the blue star on my crayon drawing of our house, with Mom and me, holding hands in the front, both with a bushel of pink flowers.

Rita Dawson walked in, smiling up at her own mother. She skipped to the desk next to mine dragging her mother behind her, the woman's heels clicking rapidly against the tiled floor. The woman smiled and laughed too, looking down at her daughter in tawny curls and a flowered jumper. "Mommy, look!" Rita sat down. The chair scraping against the floor reminded me of school days when Miss Marty would clap, clap and we'd all scramble over. Except this was just one chair. "And I have all kinds of pencils and crayons. And look! I made this drawing of us!" Her eager hands forced the paper with the crayon markings in front of her mom's face. Rita's mommy cupped her hand around Rita's chubby cheeks and kissed them. "Honey." Her mother twisted and held up the drawing to a man. "Our little girl made a family portrait of us. We'll have to hang it on the fridge."

The man smiled down at the picture. "Well, of course we'll have to. Right next to the others."

I stared hard through the filmy white of the paper, able to see the picture in reverse. A child, a woman, and a man.

I pushed the rest of the eraser garbage off the edge of the desk.

"Mommy," I said to Cici after I was called from the desk and we left. "Rita has a mommy and a daddy."

Mom pulled down the sun visor in the car and two lights illuminated her face. She brushed her fingers under her eyes and sighed. "Uh huh."

I kicked the back of the passenger seat, making a white scuffmark across the black leather. "Where's my daddy?"

"I told you before. He's d—... in heaven." She scrunched up her hair and mouth in the mirror and applied more pink color to her lips.

"But what happened to him?" I kicked the leather again, right next to the other white mark.

Mom locked eyes with me through the mirror. They were hard, icy like an evil queen. "His heart. Now,

I'm not going to talk about him anymore so if that's what you want, you can stop talking too."

My little body swelled and my chest got bigger and bigger until it got too big and too hard to keep in anymore. And the tears burst through and the cries poured out until I got smaller and smaller and wrapped my arms around myself, pretending they belonged to a man I'd never seen. And would never see.

****

"I can't believe you haven't read the whole thing yet." Drake picked up the journal that lay between us on the bed. "Don't you want to know what it says?"

I shrugged. Reading my father's words would make him real. Something my mom tried very hard to make him not be.

"Well, this is crazy. I mean, if my grandfather told me my father left a journal, I'd…" He threw his hands up in the air, along with the journal. "I just don't get it."

"You knew your father," I said, grabbing the book from him when he started to undo the clasp. "You'd know everything he had written anyway."

Drake put his hand on top of my retreating one. "You could know yours too."

"Isn't that what you're here for?" I tried to smile. It fell heavy on my face.

"That's what *you're* here for."

My heart sighed, dropping into my stomach. This could be a dream come true…or a nightmare.

I held the journal with both hands, heart somehow beating in a steady rhythm, but with a pounding force of nerves behind it. Like a heavy battering ram threatened my chest. Boom, another second—boom, another—boom. My fingers felt enormous as they worked at the clasp, like a child working at his shoes. It took three tries for my shaking hands to pull the strap tight enough to draw the bronzed spire from the hole. Drake's eyes were all over me, covering me as his body leaned in to fill the space between us. My fingers wandered over the writing on the cover. *David, 1995.*

"I was one, you know, when my dad died." My fingers lingered on the letters, waiting for a reason. To stop, to start, for everything.

"And I was two." Drake shrugged. "Open the damn book Sarah."

I cracked the journal, fast, like removing a Band-Aid. And there it was again. His words, his writing. I tried to ignore the feeling again and the similar slope of his words. To get emotional over this would be embarrassing. I couldn't help it though. I wrote like my dad. I wanted to throw open the window, stick my head out and yell, *I write like my dad! I found out today that I write like my dad. My words are like his, and his are like mine.* It was stupid, but the hot tears came anyway and rested in the corners of my eyes.

"This is about you," Drake said. He pulled the journal from my hands and read aloud. His voice in awe, but steady. I was grateful. I needed someone to make things real. Apparently, Cici and Dad were trying to get me to walk and apparently, I was 'so beautiful, *just like her mother'.*

Huh? The boom—boom—boom ended with a stuttering jerk. The rollercoaster ride stopped abruptly. *Like my mother?* "You mean they liked each other?" I tore the journal back from Drake and his wiry smile and started flipping through page after page of endearing notes of me…and Mom. 'We went to the park and Cici and Sar's eyes gleamed with excitement. Cici took her on the big slide and…', 'I came home to a mess in the kitchen today, flour all over the place and on my pretty princesses'. I looked up from the pages, completely dumbstruck, mouth wide open and the journal lying limp in my hands.

Drake laughed. "You're shocked your parents liked each other? You know where babies come from, don't you?"

I nodded, mind whirring with pictures of a loving Cici with a baby girl. With me. It was something I'd never seen before. Something I never thought I would see. And something I was sure I would never read about. "I'm just completely…I just always thought…"

Drake smiled and took the journal again. He read ahead as I processed my mother being anything other than a conceited bitch.

"Hey, Rose is in this one!" He brought the journal closer to his face and flipped back a page. "Auntie Rose called today. She didn't sound much like herself. Very cryptic. I'm going to drive up to Adams to check on her. Something about the town…I'm thinking it might be time to put her in senior living. My heart would break to do it, but with the baby, I don't have enough time to take care of her too. I'll have to see when I get there. Cici and Baby Sarah are going to spend some 'bonding time' as Ci puts it."

Ci? A cute, endearing name used for my mo—
"That's really weird. Rose has always been so with it. I can't believe your dad would have thought that sixteen years ago." He held the book out to me.

I flipped through a couple more pages, reading snippets here and there of his travels to Virginia. "Oh my God," I screamed. "He came during Settler's Days too!" Drake scooted next to me so we could read together, his arm around my back. I tracked my finger under the line as I read aloud, "I can't believe how I've missed it here. The festival, as usual, all fun and games and Auntie Rose is dragging me to everything. And when I say dragging, I mean, us running together to gobble it all up. I think she may have just needed the company. Seems as spry as ever." I giggled and threw the journal up in the air. "He likes this stuff. He loved it here."

"I told you you couldn't live in Adams and not like *this stuff.*"

I grabbed Drake by the shirt and pulled him close, crushing my lips against his. Only a few seconds later, I realized what I was doing and pulled away. *Why do I keep doing that?* I needed to get my shit together. Just because I was happy about my dad, didn't mean I had to kiss Drake. Just because I was sad about my dad before, didn't mean I needed to kiss Drake. *Why does everything I do lead to me kissing, or wanting to kiss, Drake?*

I cleared my throat. "Thank you." I grabbed the journal up again. "Thank you for making me open this."

I forced myself to meet his eyes. *He probably thinks I'm bipolar.* The tan of his cheeks turned pink. He leaned down again, eyes closing. I backed away and held out a hand to his chest. "Please...don't." I knew I had brought this on myself, keep bringing this on myself, but it needed to stop.

His head jerked up and away, his eyes flashing to my face and then down to the quilt on the bed. "Why?"

"You know, as well as me, this isn't a good idea."

He waved me away. "Yeah. No big deal. I like you and I just thought…but—What's so bad about it?"

"Oh, I don't know." I reached for his hand and then yanked it back. Probably not a good idea to make physical contact when telling a guy you didn't want to make physical contact anymore. "I live in Florida. You live in Virginia. For starters." I caught some of the hair that tickled my cheek and tucked it around my ear.

I opened up the journal again to stop from talking and to try to stop Drake from saying anything else. I stared at words, not reading anything, just seeing Drake's closing eyes and pink cheeks, feeling the way he brushed his fingers down my back earlier.

I shut my eyes tight and then opened them again. This time, thoughts cleared, I could focus on words and a symbol drawn into the book at the bottom of the page. It appeared to be a bolt of lightning with a circle around it. I wanted to concentrate on Dad's words to see what it was. At that moment though, Drake shifted on the bed and I couldn't keep my mind, and eyes, from going back to him, to his hurt face he covered up with shrugs and waves of his hand.

"But we're both here right now."

I didn't respond.

****

Drake's truck bounced along an old farming trail that weaved through the forest. Pink and orange wisps of clouds hung in the dusk sky. I sat in the passenger seat staring up at the beautiful expanse of colors, thinking of Dad and ignoring Drake's friends in the back.

Pete and a couple others messed around in the bed of the truck. They talked loud, exclaiming 'how lucky is Drake to get the only hot chick' and 'do you think they've done anything yet'. I squirmed in my seat, wishing I hadn't agreed to come to this Wiccan meeting. Drake insisted though, saying that it was cool, that there'd be a party afterwards, and of course, that my dad would have gone to it.

I didn't believe in all this crap though, and plus, it freaked me the hell out. The real reason I came, obviously, even though I half suspected Drake lied about my dad coming to these things, was for my dad. Finally, I made it to a place where he belonged. I felt like he sat next to me, moved me forward when all I really wanted to do was turn around.

When I was little, Mom went through a phase where she absolutely believed in all this metaphysical stuff. Tarot cards, psychics; you name it, she did it. She burned through tons of money to 'cleanse her soul' and 'get in touch with nature'. Blah, blah, blah.

A few years ago, Cici dragged me along with her for 'bonding' and thought it would be 'awesome' if we got a dual reading. I tried to play it off as fun until the tarot reader pulled out the death card on me. The woman swore it didn't mean anything, but I was done. Had enough. No more supernatural crap.

Except when that crap made me feel like Dad was with me apparently. Smiling at me like I always imagined when I was younger. Telling me things would be alright, even good, maybe.

A bump in the road tossed me back to reality. Looking out the windshield, the trees had grown sparse now and a vacant green area loomed a little ways in the distance. A few people stood in the clearing and others in long cloaks with their hoods up, sat in a circle. Candles flickered in the breeze, the flame bending low, bowing to the hooded party.

"Tell me again why you guys do this?" I asked, partly because I wanted to know and partly to drown out my name being thrown around back and forth behind us.

Drake couldn't be that deaf. He looked relieved to hear me talk, or maybe because I didn't react to what his friends talked about. "Adams just really embraces its…culture." Drake parked his truck next to a rusted-out old Jeep.

The truck bounced as Pete and the guys jumped out of the bed. "I thought the settlers left to get away from witchcraft."

"They did. It followed them." He smirked and pulled his ball cap down. "Weren't you paying attention last night?"

"Yesssss. I just don't understand why, if people were all afraid of witches here, do witches come around now?" I jumped out of the truck and met Drake around front.

"Why are they attracted to Salem?" Drake shrugged. "I just think Wiccans are drawn to here. It's a part of their history and ours. And listen," Drake said, putting his arm around me, "sorry about my friends' conversation back there."

"Whatever do you mean?" I nudged him. Everything fine again. I just didn't need things to get serious.

"Thanks for that." He shook his head and laughed. "Come on." He walked toward the group. "It's not polite to be late."

I saw Marlene as soon as I entered the crowd, who immediately gave me a dirty look and started whispering to her friend. "Looks like we're the talk of the town," Drake bent over and whispered. He seemed back to normal too after our conversation from earlier today. It was almost as if it didn't happen.

I didn't get to respond to him because the Wiccan meeting started. The cloaked group stood up and one of the figures began to speak. I couldn't see which one talked, since half had their backs to me and the others' heads were bent so low their hoods covered their mouths. "We will start the meeting by doing the drawing of the circle." The voice young, feminine, but powerful. "And then you will all be invited into it."

"What?" My jaw dropped. "You said we were going to a meeting, not that we'd have to participate in it."

"Just…go with it," Drake said. "It's fun."

I felt like that time I'd ate a whole bag of Swedish fish at Cynthia Cramer's thirteenth birthday party. A soaked, dead weight sloshed around in the pit of my stomach.

A cloaked figure held a candle high in the air and brought it down to light another. Drake whispered that the figure was the high priestess.

"I call upon the guardians of the east to keep watch over all who enter this circle. Let all who enter do so in perfect love and perfect trust." She kept moving, lighting different colored candles at the south, west, and north points. "The circle is cast." The robed figures lined up beside her and she said something to each one that I couldn't hear. I shuffled behind Drake, watching everyone walk around the circle as they entered.

Drake's turn came and I realized I had no idea what to say. I moved closer to hear, practically crawling up his backside, but their exchange was already done. *I guess we're going to have to wing this.*

"How do you enter this circle?" I could see now the girl was petite, with dark choppy hair that ended at her chin. "Umm…"

The girl smiled and I thought I heard her giggle. "Do you enter in perfect love and perfect trust?" she asked, peaking her eyebrow with a sly smile.

"Yes."

The girl motioned for me to step in and follow behind Drake. I wanted to yell at him for not telling me what to say, however, entering the Wiccan circle was probably not the right time.

The petite witch moved to the middle. Everybody stared as she lowered her hood. "We gather together on this, the celebration of our coven and its freedom to practice magic without fear. We gather together to honor the memory of those that we have lost to ignorance." Her voice a melody of rhythm, the wind, candles, everything seemed to move at her pace, her pitch. "We gather together to unite our friendships and welcome new ones."

The melodic voice poured into me, sprouting goosebumps and tingling my limbs as my brain lost all sense of worry and inhibition. It felt almost as if I were transported back to the sixties and became some stoner hippie without a care in the world.

I liked it.

"I call upon the goddess Isis in your many forms..."

I lurched forward, a pressure on my shoulders shoving me. I tried to resist, digging my feet in the ground, attempting to step backwards. All over my body, tingling flesh weighted me forward like a thousand hands forcing me to move. Beside and behind me, no one touched me. No one was even that close except for Drake. I looked around the circle and nobody noticed what was happening. They stared straight ahead at the one who formed the circle.

I tried to kneel, to fall on purpose like the first time I went skiing and couldn't stop. My muscles wouldn't obey. They moved forward another step. I shut my eyes and concentrated, forcing myself back, digging deep into my core and willing my body to move. It did.

Two steps in reverse and I was back into the circle. Drake stood again to my right, staring straight ahead, still watching the girl, never even noticing what just went down.

I urged in a few uneasy breaths. The hooded witches stared at the ground. As I watched them, one by one, they looked in my eyes and lowered their hoods. Their eyes rolled into the filmy white behind, two moon spheres on each witch staring straight at me. Glowing red emanated from deep within them, like a red beacon through dense fog. My eyes narrowed, even though every sense in my body urged me to flinch, to close my eyes and wake up in Neverland. I stood, marbleized like a great goddess statue.

Light wind tracked a hair across my face and burned my eyes, but still I did not blink. The red flickered brighter and brighter until it singed the cloudy white.

A lightning bolt encased in a circle. *The same symbol from Dad's journal.*

All force gave way within me and I toppled over, landing outside of the circle and onto the crunchy grass. Even with my eyes closed, I saw nothing but the symbol etched there. It flamed out, the red reaching for me. I screamed.

A hand came down on my shoulder, startling me. I tensed for another scream. *Flames. No more flames.*

"Shh." The voice was calming. "Shh, Sarah. It's okay."

My heartbeat slowed, eyes blinking a few times, and then opened. Drake's face hovered above me as his hand brushed a few strands of hair off my forehead. Eyes sick with worry, he peered down, crouching on all fours now like a kneeling angel.

My eyes burned as tears rushed there. "I saw...I saw..."

"It's okay, Sarah. I'll take you to Rose's, okay? Everything's fine." He promised me.

People crowded around. When the ones with the hoods popped into view, I dug my heels into the ground again and pushed back. "No...no."

Drake forced my shoulders onto the grass.

One of the hooded figures towered over me and threw back the black cloth of the hood. "She broke the circle!" Her mouth white-lipped, the girl reached out, tore an object from the high priestess' hands, and came at me. I tried to lunge backward. Drake still held me down though. An angel of captivity. I bucked, but nothing happened. I had no strength to fight.

I saw the girl clearly now, the object glinting in her hands. It was Jennie.

She came at me with a knife.

ERIN BUTLER

Chapter Eight

1639

*The signs will be there for all to read
when man shall do most heinous deed.
Man will ruin kinder lives
by taking them as to their wives.*

*And murder foul and brutal deed
when man will only think of greed.
Women they shall falsely accuse
so their suffering will bemuse.*

After the steps of her mother left the bedroom and before the full morning rays of sun shone through the window, Isabella sat at her desk, waiting.

The picture in Isabella's head repeated over and over. Mrs. Shipton with her fire eyes blazed before her, darkening as her singsong voice repeated these lines, casting her prophecy like the weaver pieces together his threads, each string working together to complete the vision.

During the night, she convinced herself of it being a dream. A dream it must be. What evil force could make her lose her senses, not sure, if she woke or slept?

Isabella calmed herself by thinking of Thomas. He would surely see no reason to be scared. One word from him would silence her fears.

The ink from her quill stained a circle around the point, which still rested on paper. The dark liquid spread outward, tainting the perfectly lined prose. Eyes transfixed on the door, Isabella stood from her perch. Her legs pricked, beginning at her thighs and creeping down to her toes. Splotches of stings bloomed just beneath her clammy skin. With each step, the pain flared.

"Mother," she called out, "I wrote this for you." She looked down, not knowing why she spoke. It was a letter for Thomas in her hands, not for her mother.

A scream pierced the air. Her scream.

The prophecy Mrs. Shipton sang last night was written on the paper she clasped in her hands. It was written on her parchment, on her desk, and in her own hand.

> *Women they shall falsely accuse*
> *so their suffering will bemuse.*

The door clattered open. Mrs. Lynne rushed through once again. Isabella dropped the paper and staggered back, her feet hit the stool and it banged backward onto the wood floor.

"Isabella? What is the matter?"

She gaped at her mother. Words did not come. How could she explain about Mrs. Shipton? "I did not write that."

"Write what, Dear?"

"I did not write the nonsense on that piece of parchment."

Mrs. Lynne hugged her tight, rubbing circles on her back. "You have had a rough night, Daughter. You are not needed for chores this morning." She kissed her head. "Go back to sleep."

Mr. Lynne's uneasy step came in. "What is the matter here?"

"Isabella has had nightmares and I think she may not be feeling well today. She says that she did not write."

"Write what?"

"Father." Isabella approached him, hands shaking. "There is writing on that parchment. How it got there, I know not. But it was not of my doing."

She pointed to the paper on the floor and Mr. Lynne bent over to retrieve it. He read the poem and looked up from the paper at his trembling child. "What is this?"

"Mrs. Shipton has written it."

"Mrs. Shipton?" His eyes narrowed to slits. "How did she come to be in your room?"

Tears poured from Isabella's eyes. "She was not, Sir. The nightmare I had last night. She was in it and she said those words. She sang them around a fire."

"That is just a dream."

"She is a witch."

"Isabella!" Mr. Lynne's voice bellowed. "Do not throw out accusations. There is too much of that at present."

"But Father, I—"

Mrs. Lynne stepped forward, reaching out. "What does it say?"

He snatched the paper from her reach. "'Tis nothing, just nonsense."

Mr. Lynne took one last look at the two of them and turned on his heels. Out the door he went and into the main hall. He threw the piece of parchment on the hearth and watched it shrivel up and burn.

ERIN BUTLER

Chapter Nine

Present Day

Jennie grabbed the hilt of the knife with both hands and slashed down. The knife sunk into the earth right off my left hand.

I hurled myself backwards. "Wait! Don't move," she yelled. Pushing Drake out of the way, Jennie brought the knife up again and swung it down into the earth on my other side.

"What the hell?" Drake charged between us, holding a strong, muscled hand in front of Jennie's chest.

She stared him down. "She broke the circle. Now we have to repair it. *Take her out of it*." She waved the knife toward me. "*Now.*"

The leader with the choppy hair stepped up and placed a hand on the other girl's shoulder. "Jennie, these are guests. They don't know about the sanctity of the circle."

"She needs to leave." The witch's stare fixed on me. Beads of sweat formed on her hairline and her fair skin sponged into pink circles. She didn't appear any different from earlier today. Same bitchy face and snarky attitude.

"Don't worry. *She* is," I said, placing both hands underneath me. With Drake's help, I moved away from the circle and out onto the fringes. Jennie and the leader hovered over the spot where I stood, the palm reader spying over the leader's shoulder as they spouted some weird incantations and used a candle to make the circle whole again. The leader smiled at me several times. I didn't care. I just wanted to go.

"You okay?" Drake whispered. He held me in a hug still, arms completely engulfing me. I felt like a small doll in his embrace.

"Yeah," I choked out. "I'm good."

"What happened?"

I shook my head. I wasn't about to tell him I was going crazy. "I don't...like supernatural stuff."

"It is pretty interesting though, isn't it?"

"Huh? Scary witches and spells?"

"No." Drake drew me away at arm's length. "Those stories Courtney told us about the first settlers." His eyes sparkled.

I racked my brain. I didn't remember any stories, only cloaked figures with white eyeballs. "I couldn't really hear her talking."

"You probably drowned her out. Forty-five minutes is pretty long."

"Forty-five minutes?" *Holy crap. Are you kidding me?* I thought I had only been here for ten.

A tap on my shoulder made me whirl around to find Courtney smiling again. The cloak gone, shed somewhere in the Wiccan magic world, the high priestess almost looked normal.

"Hey, I wanted to come over and introduce myself." Her voice tuned so much softer than it sounded from within the circle. I wouldn't even recognize the two voices as coming from the same person. "I'm Courtney."

"I'm Sarah." I tugged on Drake's shirt and took a step toward the truck.

Courtney kept talking. "I've seen you around, just haven't had the chance yet to say hi. You're staying with Rose, aren't you? She's such a sweet woman."

I peeked at Drake who hadn't budged an inch.

"Are you okay by the way?"

"Yeah. Fine." I crossed my arms in front of me.

"Sometimes the energy in a circle can be too much for newbs." Courtney shrugged. "But Jennie shouldn't have acted that way. She's new here. She doesn't get how we do things yet."

"Yeah, you better watch her," Drake said. "She's strange. She said something earlier today too. To Sarah, when we were at the festival."

"I'll keep my eye on her."

This witch acted too perky to be anything but nice. I dropped my arms and rejoined Drake. Despite her eccentric behavior, and the fact that she practiced witchcraft, I actually liked Courtney. Could have maybe even been friends with her. She stayed a while and talked, eager to show us some things and answer my long list of questions.

When I asked if she did magic, the witch just smiled and said, "Some may call it that. We cast spells during rituals, usually calling on a certain god or goddess to help bring about physical changes in our world. We like to think of Wicca as working with nature though, not particularly magic."

I nodded, liking that idea better than the vision I had stuck in my head from all those scary movies like "The Craft". "Do you know about the history of witchcraft? Like, did convicted witches really get burned at the stake?"

"Actually, it's a common misconception. The majority of accused women were actually hung. There are only a few infamous cases of witches being burned. Some of them just happened to be in this village. Were you at the opening night ceremony?"

"Yes."

Courtney leaned in closer, her smile filling the lower half of her face. "That was the reenactment of one of *our* ancestors. She actually *burned* on a stake."

My jaw dropped and a nervous twinge fluttered in my stomach. "Wait. A reenactment? I thought you guys were just burning some doll that represented fear of witches and witchcraft."

The witch shook her head eagerly. "Nope. She represented one of the witches that burned here."

I stared off to where the circle had been. The candles were blown out immediately afterward and now the clearing was as dark as the night sky had become. Everyone went to their cars and started turning their lights on. I, of course, just happened to be looking at one when the light gleamed, piercing my eye.

Twisting away and blinking, the lights caught on something else shiny. I blinked a few more times, trying to get my sight back and realized the shiny something hung around Marlene's neck. It was the same symbol.

"What is that symbol I keep seeing?" I asked, gesturing toward Marlene.

"What symbol?"

"It has like a jagged line, a lightning bolt, maybe, with a circle around it."

Courtney's eyes darkened, like she stared out into an oncoming storm. "No one would wear that here."

"What is it?"

Courtney blinked. "It's a common misconception. We work with nature. It's not particularly magic."

"You said that already. The symbol. What's that symbol mean?" I pointed again to Marlene's neck.

"What symbol?"

"The one with the jagged line—"

"Oh," Courtney laughed, "that one. It's just a symbol. Means nothing really."

"But you—"

"Are you ready to go?" Drake laid his hand at the small of my back.

I jumped at his touch, but nodded anyway, watching full smiles engross both Courtney and Drake's faces like a painted on clowns. This town was so weird. *Twilight Zone* mixed with *Leave It To Beaver* and everyone had Botox smiles. Anything could happen and people would still be smiling.

I turned to leave and saw Jennie watching us. She motioned with her head to a spot behind a small car. When I didn't move, she waved her hand at me to come over.

Yeah. Right.

"Goodbye, Sarah," Courtney shouted. "I hope to see you again."

The truck lurched and bounced on the dirt road back to the highway. Pete and the others stayed. They shook their heads and waved Drake away, all while eyeing me and sending curious glances my way.

"Drake, if I told you something, would you think I was weird?"

"Probably. If it was something weird."

I stared out the window as the forest broke and the concrete of the road soldiered through it. He smiled over at me. I didn't return it. "There was a symbol in my dad's journal."

"Uh huh," Drake urged.

"It caught my eye and then tonight, at the meeting, I saw that same symbol. It scared me...almost." The highway had veins of cracks splitting the road.

"Hey," he said, peeling my fingers off the upholstery of the truck. "I'm sure it's nothing. I just don't think you're used to all this...stuff. It's getting to you."

"Maybe."

"Why don't you talk to your mom about it?" I looked over at him, face drawn. *He must be joking.* "Okay, well, talk to Rose."

"Maybe I will." That sounded like a much sounder plan.

****

I found Rose as soon as Drake dropped me off. "I'm glad you're here. I want to talk to you if you have time." She sat at the dining room table, a newspaper spread out before her. One of the nasty coffees steamed from a mug she cupped in her hands. "No festival duties tonight?" I asked when she made no reply.

"None tonight."

"I want to know about my dad."

"What don't you know?" The steam curled up and around Rose's face, misting her in white shadows.

"Everything."

"Hmm," she snickered, "I always thought your mom was kind of a bitch."

My mouth dropped, a laugh spilling out. Soon, both of us laughed. I pulled out a chair across from Aunt Rose and sat. "I don't know why she doesn't want me to know."

"Probably because she feels threatened." Rose took a sip of her coffee and set it down again. "David was such a great person. It was too bad about the accident." Rose peeled up the corner of the paper and started to turn the page.

"Accident? I thought he had a heart attack."

Rose dropped the page, eyes glossing over. "Is that what they deemed it?" She shook her head, the black liquid rippling her reflection. "Then it was because of the accident he had a heart attack."

"My mom didn't tell me."

"She didn't tell me either." Rose stared down at the same article, eyes moving across the words.

"What was the accident?"

Rose spoke in a controlled monotone, relaying everything she knew, which wasn't much. My mind whirred. Pictures of scenes I never saw flashed in and out of my mind like the shutter of a camera. Every detail Rose gave me, I relived it, a ghost next to my father as he lived out his last seconds.

No. It couldn't be like that.

"Do you think I could see your father's journal?" Rose asked.

I nodded and pointed upstairs, my body robotic. "In my room."

Rose's head bowed and hung over. Her shoulders shook and shining tears dripped one-by-one off the end of her nose.

I grabbed her hand. "What else?"

"Your mom wouldn't let me do anything. She came up here, took over, and had his body out of Adams so fast I didn't even know what happened. I was still in shock." Her choked words melted to sobs. "I couldn't even go to the funeral I was in such a state."

My heart pounded in my chest with all the fury I'd buried deep, but I forced a small smile. "I read some of his journal entries where he talks about you." I patted the old woman's hand. "He loved you very much."

"You read it?" Rose's head cocked up, her face cinched and loaded.

"Some of it. I just got up the nerve to today."

"Can I read it first?" Rose grabbed my hands and squeezed them.

I hesitated. My aunt's face crumpled all over again though, balled up like a paper bag, tears streaming out. One second scared or jealous or some other mixed up emotion, and another, alone. Maybe the inability to understand my feelings was a passed down trait. That made me less psychotic, didn't it? "Sure, Aunt Rose. You can read it."

Rose sighed. "Thank you, honey. Thank you." She reached out and I went willingly into her arms, a weight lifting and flying from my heart. I hugged someone my father loved.

She gave me one last squeeze and we broke away, each of us rubbing our eyes with the backs of our hands. I ran to my room. The journal lay on the bed, open to the place where the symbol was drawn into it.

Rose's steps echoed in the stairway. I couldn't help myself. I read the passage next to the symbol. *Today I found this painted on the library floor. Auntie Rose kneeled in the middle of it and I thought she was having a seizure because she shook violently. As soon as I stepped into the chalked-in circle though, she stopped and scolded me for coming into the library. I hope she's not sick. Ever since her neighbor died in that car accident, I think she's been losing touch with reality.*

"There you are dear. Did you find it?" I turned. My aunt's waiting hand was stretched out before me.

I gave it to her, a smile planted on my face. The poor woman was being brave. Rose started to turn away. I stopped her. "I need to talk to Drake."

"I think that's a great idea, Sarah."

"Why didn't *he* tell me what happened?"

Rose clasped the journal to her chest. "It is possible he may not even know. Don't be too harsh on him now."

I clenched my hands at my sides, feeling the loss of the book and of a truth I didn't see for a lie. "His grandfather killed someone. Why wouldn't he know?"

Chapter Ten

1639

Isabella skirted the crop line that ran along the road with a handful of purple and yellow wild flowers she thought her mother would like. The breeze of the evening air cooled her face. She took her bonnet off and held on to the tie as it trailed behind. Leaning her head back, she watched as the first stars sparkled in the dark blue measureless sky that would soon be turning black.

When she woke earlier, her mother released her from her duties and begged her to stay outside, to breathe in the fresh air, and to not think of evil doings. The fresh air revived her, but it was the thinking of evil she could not contain. It surrounded her, engulfed her into a never-ending nightmare. Every cry of the bird or chirping insect started her heart thumping as if the creatures of the night waited for her wherever she walked. She peeked behind every tree and bush, fearful of what lay ahead.

The sun descended further, the stars bright now in the sky. Isabella retreated back to the house. She passed the edge of the barn and saw a figure walking up the dirt path. He was yet too far away to identify.

As she turned to open the cottage door, the man waved, motioning for her to stop.

Isabella's heart sped. It was Thomas. She could tell by his wide-brimmed hat and breeches.

She stared at the ground, twisting her black shoes into the soil while she waited. Her cheeks burned despite the cool breeze.

"Good day, Isabella."

"Good day, Sir." It was seeing him outside, and not in the sanctity of the barn that caused her formal greeting. She slipped into it as normal, like when they greeted one another on Sunday, or out on the town streets.

She looked up when he did not speak. His face drawn and grave, almost disappointed. "I must talk with your father."

"What is it?"

Thomas shoved his fingers into his breeches and sighed. "My father wants his help with the search parties."

Isabella gasped. "The search parties?" She shook her head. "He will not like to, Thomas."

"I know—"

"Cannot you ask your father to excuse him?"

"I tried, but he is the magistrate and this is what he wishes."

"Might he ask someone else?" Isabella stumbled through her words, grasping for a different solution.

"He is asking everyone. Those who do not help will be considered suspicious."

Isabella staggered backward, dropping the flowers from her hands, and almost fell when her foot caught the rock on the side of the door. Thomas reached out to steady her. "You do not understand what it has been like here. Mother Shipton…" Her words dissolved into a choked sob.

"What of Mrs. Shipton?"

"I think she is a witch. I dreamt of her. A nightmare." Isabella's words poured from her mouth like a gushing stream. "She bid me come to her in the woods. She stood by a fire, singing incantations. Then, she turned to me and said, 'I see you.' Her eyes like fire." Isabella finished breathless, but upon seeing the doubt in his eyes, she started again. "And you know she is a medicine woman. She mixes herbs and plants, and cures the ailments of others. Does not that ability recommend her?"

"If that were true, every woman would be thought a witch. Has not your mother taught you something of medicine?"

"But of course." Isabella took a steadying breath. "Pray, listen, Thomas. Her knowledge is great. She has powers."

"My father does not think—"

"That is not the worst part!" Isabella reached out and grabbed his wrist. "This morning, I woke up to find a piece of parchment on my desk that I did not write. The words are not mine. It was the song that came from her lips."

Thomas' eyes burned into hers. "What has become of the parchment?" His arms went rigid and she dropped him from her grasp.

"I do not know. I believe my father has got rid of it."

His shoulders sagged. "Good. That is exactly what I would have done." He reached for her hand and then let it drop in the space between them. "Do not speak of this to anybody."

Isabella shook her head. "I would not."

Thomas gazed out at the road. "My father does not believe Mrs. Shipton is a witch. Others share your fear though." He took in a deep breath. "Mrs. Crawford was caught stealing today."

Isabella's mouth fell open. "Who caught her?"

"No one. 'Tis said that Mrs. Owens paid a visit to Mother Shipton and within the half-hour, Mrs. Crawford came running down the street, singing."

"Singing?" Isabella stared at Thomas, refusal darkening her eyes.

"Yes, I was right there to see. She repeated this song over and over. 'I stole my neighbors' smock and petticoat, I am a thief and here I show it.'"

"Might it be Mrs. Crawford is unwell?"

"I am sure she is. However, that is of no matter. She is locked in the stocks as we speak." Thomas dug his foot into the earth, his face long and drawn. "'Tis not the worst of the news. All the townspeople believe Mrs. Shipton is the reason for our misfortunes. The crops failing. The stricken children. I agree that she has powers, Isabella. We all know that. All but my father, the magistrate. Who has not gone to her for medicines and such? And why else would Mrs. Crawford admit to stealing the petticoat, if she indeed did steal it?"

"Perhaps Mrs. Crawford felt guilt. She wanted penance."

"You were not there to see. Mrs. Crawford wore a strange expression as if she was not trying to do what she did." Thomas mimicked the townswoman, staring at his arms, his jaw slack and eyes full of wonder. "She kept looking at her legs and arms like she could not understand why they moved. And all the while, she was singing that song. Everyone from town is in an uproar because of it. They are all scared."

"What is the magistrate going to do?"

"Nothing!" Thomas' hands clenched into fists. "He believes it not."

"Shh," Isabella silenced him. She held her hand aloft; the floorboards creaked inside.

"Be careful of her," Thomas whispered.

The door opened and Mr. Lynne stepped out. Isabella bowed to Thomas. "Here is my father now, Mr. Ludington."

"Thank you, Miss Lynne." Thomas bowed back and then straightened his jacket as Mr. Lynne approached them.

Isabella excused herself. She entered the house, her head hung low over her shoulders. Her father would not be pleased when he came in.

"Isabella," her mother called. "I wish to speak with you."

She came into the hall, her hands still around the bonnet, twisting and untwisting the ties. "Of course, Mother."

Mrs. Lynne set aside her sewing. "Who is here?"

"Thomas Ludington." She could feel her heartbeat as her mother's eyes bore into her. A flint of recognition crossed her face.

"I need you to tell me what they are speaking of."

"I am sure I do not know."

"Do not lie to me." Mrs. Lynne stood, her hands quivering as she gestured to her daughter. "You have been seeing him, without chaperone, and in these dark times." Her mother stepped in front of her, face red and shaking. "You will bring suspicion down on your whole family!"

Mrs. Lynne raised her hand and struck her daughter's face with trembling fingers. Isabella's own hands flew to her cheek as the pain swelled. Tears dripped from her mother's eyes as she turned, chin up, and walked steady back to her sewing.

ERIN BUTLER

Chapter Eleven

Present Day

"Tell me you didn't know. Just tell me you didn't know."

Throw me in the loony bin. The drive over here had been one heck of a mental whiplash. First, I was sure Drake knew all along and was trying to make it up to me by liking me. As crazy as that sounds. Then, I was sure he didn't know anything and that his grandfather was a lying, skuzzy old geezer.

Drake swayed on the doorstep of his house, one hand still on the doorknob, the other wiping sleep from his eyes. "Sarah?" His shirt was off and his chest was etched in the glow of the moon.

I held my lips in a tight line, pushing the pain deeper inside. My fingers still pinched the key to the Escalade, pinched the metal so hard I was getting a cramp. "Please tell me you didn't know."

"What's wrong? What's happened?" His sandy hair stuck up in all directions. A bang sounded from upstairs. "It's okay, Grandpa," he yelled, then stepped out onto the porch and shut the door. His eyes flicked to the second story again as he let out a sigh before turning his dragging body toward me.

Anger ticked away inside. Heat in my veins spread through my entire body, waiting to ignite. "Your grandfather killed my father."

"What?" His eyes narrowed.

"Your grandfather killed my father," I repeated, trying to keep myself together.

"I heard you. I just don't think you know what you're talking about."

"It's true. Rose told me." Despite the fact I willed myself to keep the tears in, they spilled over, running down my face.

"You said your dad had a heart attack."

Drake reached out, but I pulled back. "Apparently, a heart attack brought on by the fact that your grandfather was about to run him over."

Drake's mouth pursed. He shook his head from side to side and his eyes clouded over. "That's ridiculous. I would have heard about it."

"Ridiculous? You think this is ridiculous? What happened—?"

"There's only one way to find out *what happened*."

"Exactly." I pushed Drake out of the way and marched toward the stairs. "Where's your—?"

Drake grabbed my hand and held it. "No. Not happening." His grip tightened around my wrist when I tried to pull away. "My grandpa's sick. I'm not taking this to him if it's bullshit."

I hesitated, looking back at the porch stairs and then to Drake again. His eyes had the same apprehension in them when he floated above me at the Wiccan meeting. His bare chest expanding to capacity every time he took a breath. "But Rose told me." My voice came out small, certainly not boiling over in rage anymore.

He dropped my arm and sat on the step, head in his hands. "Why wouldn't she tell *me*? Why wouldn't my grandfather have told *me*?"

"Nobody knew I existed," I offered. The muscles in his back pulled taut. "They probably thought everything was all over. Done with. Why upset you?"

He looked up, eyebrows drawn together. The muscles in his shoulders and arms thick and rigid. "So why are you telling me?"

"Because I have to know."
****

"This is the best you came up with?" I pulled into a parking spot in front of the Adams Police Station, a dinky one-story concrete box with barely any windows.

"They'll have records on everything. You want to know what really happened to your dad? This is where we start." Drake hopped out of the Escalade and continued to the building door and through it before I even turned off the ignition. *Someone wound him up tight*, I thought.

Oh yeah, that was me.

I mimicked him, except I slammed the door much harder than he did. A voice rang through the station as I entered. "Hey, Rudy, get me the Perkins-Connors file from the back. '94, isn't that right, Connors?"

Drake turned to me and I nodded. "That's right, Pauly," he said. The tag stuck out of the shirt he hastily threw on after he got his bright idea to come down here in the middle of the night.

"It's Officer Pike now, Connors." The tall, wiry guy playfully punched Drake in the arm.

Drake smirked. "Yeah, yeah."

I strode up to them, searing my eyes into Drake's. "Hey, hey, what do we have here?" Officer Pike asked.

"Pauly, this is Sarah *Perkins.*"

"O-kay then." He averted his eyes and searched the back for Rudy. An older, rounder cop came around the corner. "Here we go," Pauly said, taking the manila folder from his friend. He opened the folder up and looked through the contents. "Yeah, didn't even know this happened, 'cept I happened to run across it one day and the name caught my eye." He took a few papers out of the folder and placed them upside down on the counter.

"What are—?" I started to ask.

"Pictures," Drake snapped. I took a step back, knocked out of whack by his anger. The next second, he turned to smile at Pauly. "Thanks for this man." Drake bounced the folder off the edge of the counter and walked toward the little sitting area, which boasted orange upholstered chairs with ripped seams and a fake fern plant. "Listen, before we open this—"

"Just give me the damn folder, Drake." I ripped it out of his hands and plopped down in one of the faded chairs. This whole town needed to be freakin' medicated.

"Hey," Drake said, placing his palm on top of the folder as I tried to open it. He waited until I lifted my gaze to him. "I just wanted to say, whatever is in here, I swear I didn't know about it." He took his hand away, his eyes searching for something in mine. "And whatever *is* in there, won't bring him back either."

I rolled my eyes and opened the manila folder. It only took a minute to read through the report. The coroner was clear, patient had a heart attack and lost consciousness before the vehicle struck him. Could have happened seconds or hours after.

I sighed, relieved, but still hurt as my heart tore at the seams. I flipped through the other reports, just grazing them, when a half sheet of paper fluttered to the ground. Drake took the folder as I bent forward to retrieve it. "I'm sorry, Sarah, but this—"

"Oh my god." My whole body convulsed as I stared down at the paper lying on the floor. A sketch on cloudy paper rested among the dirty, white-speckled linoleum tiles.

The lightning symbol with the circle.

Chapter Twelve

1639

Mr. Lynne returned to the house with Thomas in tow. The younger man nodded at Isabella, as was polite, and then kept his eyes to the floor. Mr. Lynne glanced at his daughter too and then found his wife still sitting by the hearth with her sewing. He looked as if he knew not what to do. Every time his eyes slid over Isabella, she cocked her head to the side, pretending to look at the far wall so she could hide her face.

His eyes were sharp and cold as icicles as they bore into the room. Isabella caught a tiny movement from Thomas as she stared at the wall. The young man cleared his throat. "Sir, my father is waiting…" Mr. Lynne's heavy sigh interrupted him and the loud knock of his work boots on the wood floors silenced the friendly command.

"I am sor—" Thomas' step forward halted and he fell back into his place, eyes on the floorboards as Mrs. Lynne stood from her perch. Thomas' face reddened. He did not know she was there.

Her face was completely calm now. No wetness gleamed from her cheeks or eyes. She fretted with her lip, trying, but failing to mask her worried face. "But what of us?" She walked up to Thomas, standing before him with her hands outstretched. "We have no others here. 'Tis just Isabella and I." Her quavering voice lifted Thomas' eyes to hers. His features melted into limp clay.

Head bowing below his shoulders, the slow footsteps of Mr. Lynne's heavy boots once again sounded as he came up behind his wife and laid a comforting hand around her shoulders. Isabella could not tell if her father pulled her mother back or if she did so under his protecting hand. Soon all three of them stood together, facing Thomas.

His head perked again, but his features still fell loose on his face. He looked more like a boy than ever. Isabella wanted to reach out, to hold him and tell him none of this was his fault.

"Thomas assures me that the hunting parties do not last very long. The evil ones come out when the moon is high, neither before, nor after." Mr. Lynne looked back at the boy; an unpardonable smile sneaked its way across his lips. "And if I have my chance to rid this town of *true* evil, I shall not hesitate."

Isabella's mother wrapped her arms around him, sobbing a little into his shoulder. Isabella watched her father stroke her mother's long hair. Thomas tried a few times to catch his lover's eye. She ignored him, all of them. She retreated to the corner of the room and looked past all the pain she could be sharing, should be sharing. Her cheek still burned underneath her skin and she let the anger swarm her.

Mr. Lynne whispered in his wife's ear and then moved to Isabella. His reassuring smile faltered when he got closer. He took her face in his hands and peered at her cheek. She flushed and tried to turn away. His thumb stroked her swollen skin and Isabella could not help but wince.

Frowning, he turned to his wife who stuck her chin in the air, face resolute, though fresh, wet tears adorned her cheeks. Thomas caught the exchange and he moved closer. His face transfigured in pain and even though he still stood, his whole body buckled into itself, shrunk with the weight of despair.

With great care, her father kissed her aching cheek and looked deep in her eyes. His face solemn, but heroic. His eyes said what his words could not. An apology. For her throbbing cheek? For his future absence? For her unacknowledged love? She knew not. Isabella pushed past him and escaped to her room.

****

A short time after the men left, a loud knock rapped on the door to the Lynne home. Isabella stiffened, her quill ceased to move across the journal paper in mid-word.

Voices.

Isabella listened, waiting to hear shouted orders from her mother. The words exchanged were in whispers though. Hardly audible from within the confines of Isabella's bedroom. She moved to the door and cupped her ear against the wood.

Women voices.

Isabella turned the knob and, as slow as the worm crawls in the summer heat, she inched the door open. Her heart quickened with the ever-growing sliver of light. As the picture before her appeared in full view, she gasped and grabbed hold of the door casing lest she might fall.

She stood there—the witch—just before her in the kitchen, towering over her mother with a crooked grin. Isabella's step faltered and she tripped back into the room. Her footfall sounded heavily on the creaking board in the middle and her mother's head snapped to look at her.

"Mrs. Shipton?" Isabella drew in a ragged breath and blood raced through her veins. She searched the little crevices of the room, looking for something, anything to use as a weapon against the evil thing.

"Isabella, calm yourself," her mother implored. "Please." Her eyes were etched in anger.

"Why is she here?" Her voice came out terse, but wavered despite herself.

"Dear Isabella," Mrs. Shipton exclaimed. "You are getting prettier and prettier by the day." Her constant haggard features wrinkled even more. "Pray tell me, what is your secret? Do you possess those womanly powers that most artless women crave?" Mrs. Shipton's gaze sliced through the young girl. Isabella reached back and ran her hand over her long braid, but Mrs. Shipton's eyes did not follow. They stared into her, not at her, reading her, seeking all the good inside and scoffing at it, burying it with her fire eyes.

A tremor raked her body. What could Mrs. Shipton be about? Saying those things to her?

"I assure you I possess no powers but those traits which my mother and father have given me." Isabella doubted the old hag could say the same.

Mrs. Shipton laughed, laying a hand over her middle. "Oh Isabella, I see that the dire times have reached your ears." The old woman looked back to her mother and frowned. "I did not mean powers such as Isabella took me to mean." Mrs. Shipton waved her hands, shooing away evil like she would scare away a fly. As if this all meant nothing to her, as if everything meant nothing to her. "I meant womanly powers such as beauty and grace, which most insipid, ugly women want. You know, much like myself. My mother and father were not as kind to me as yours have been to you."

With narrowed eyes, Isabella walked up to her two elders. She leaned forward a little on her toes, tipped her chin and then looked down, masking the rapid beat of her heart. "You must know, Mrs. Shipton…You must see that you cannot be here."

"Isabella!" Mrs. Lynne's hands clenched the sides of her apron.

Isabella did not spare a glance to her mother. "My father is away on a witch hunting party—"

"As is Mr. Shipton. The same one, I am sure."

Isabella fell back on her heels. "I must ask you to leave. Three women, alone…at night…it looks suspicious."

Mrs. Lynne, prepared to yell at her daughter again, choked back her words. Mrs. Shipton gazed at her and then nodded. "Hmm. Perhaps you are right, young one." She turned to leave, but before the door closed behind her, she looked back in and said, "Perhaps you should take as much caution with *other* villagers who come visiting at night."

As the door shut, Isabella followed after, making sure the latch secured itself in the resting place. Her hand lingered there and she pressed her forehead against the cool of the wood door.

"Isabella, my, what is a matter with you? You cannot behave like that."

Voice quieted by her churning mind, Isabella said, "She is evil ma'am. Please."

Mrs. Lynne shook her head and snapped out, "You believe she is evil because she gave you away." Isabella spun around, her mouth open in surprise. "Yes. She is the one who informed me of you and Thomas meeting secretly."

Isabella shook her head as if the force of her disagreement would help sway her mother. "She is evil and I know it." Mrs. Lynne sighed and leaned against the wall, her face toward the rafters. Isabella clamored over, stepping closer to her mother. "She did not hurt you?"

"I am well."

"But she leaned over you here. The look on her face…" Isabella's words trailed off, her mother already shaking her head in disagreement.

"We were just talking. She wanted to trade crop. Pretty Isabella…" her mother slouched down in a chair, confusion racking her face. Her brows drew together as she studied her daughter. "Why do you think this of Mrs. Shipton?"

Isabella's heart stuttered to a stop, like the last gallop of horse's hooves on packed dirt. "I have heard stories." Her terror let her speak the words. Too afraid for her family to lie to her mother now.

"From Thomas, I suppose." She looked deep into her daughter's eyes. Isabella could not tell what the look meant. It wavered between horror and sadness.

"'Tis true, Mother, from Thomas Ludington. We—"

Mrs. Lynne interrupted. "Mrs. Shipton has told me of you and Thomas Ludington."

Isabella's eyebrows arched. "I am not sure how Mrs. Shipton would know of anything."

"She said she saw you talking." Her mother patted the stool next to her. "She meant to put me on my guard. She agrees that this is merely a silly dalliance, but Isabella, you cannot be too careful."

Isabella's heart ached. *Silly dalliance?*

"If Mrs. Shipton was able to see you two together, any townsperson might have. If the wrong person spied you…"

"I love him," Isabella choked out, her face drowning in sadness.

She wanted to say more, needed to say more, but her mother began again, "Then why has he not proposed? Has he spoken to his parents?" A tear streamed down the pink cheek of Isabella. Mrs. Lynne stood up straighter and said in clear, commanding words, "You are not to see Thomas Ludington again."

Chapter Thirteen

Present Day

I eyed the two police officers. They joked at the counter, engrossed in a conversation about the older man's wife and her less than spectacular cooking skills. I slipped my phone from my pocket and snapped a picture of the symbol.

Drake's eyes flicked to the laughing men. "You can't do that," he whispered.

"Stop me." The warning shot off my tongue, doused in sarcasm.

I imbedded the image in a text and sent it to Mom, along with **TX for telling me dad got RAN OVER! Does this symbol mean ne thing to u??**

I flipped the phone shut and waited. Drake nudged me with a piece of paper, the corner jabbed the fleshy skin of my bicep. "You need to see this."

His eyes darkened over as I took the paper. He watched the officers now too.

A SYMBOL (ATTACHED IN FORM 3-E) WAS FOUND ON THE LEFT BREAST. SYMBOL UNKNOWN AND CONCLUDED NOT IN INTEREST TO THE INVESTIGATION.

Not in interest to the investigation? These hicks don't even know how to do their jobs. I jumped up, grabbed everything from Drake's hands and threw it at the two cops. Sheets of paper spiraled through the air in disarray. They caught air underneath them, changed direction, and then losing the unseen forces keeping them aloft, sunk to the floor. "What the fuck is this?" I yelled.

Drake scrambled up behind me. "Sarah," he warned.

"No…no…I want to know what this is." I slapped the drawing of the symbol down on the counter in front of the startled cops. "I keep seeing this everywhere." I jabbed at the paper, pointing, like taunting a coiled snake.

"Miss…"

My phone buzzed and I opened it, holding out a finger to the cops. **I can't believe ur bitch of an aunt told u that.**

"Miss?" the older police officer started again, teeth clenched together.

I motioned with my finger again for them to give me one second. **Screw you MOM!!!!!!!!,** I texted back, and pushed the power button so hard I thought I might break the key before the phone turned off. The tip of my thumb turned white while the blood pooled underneath the nail.

"Drake," Pauly warned. "You might want to…"

Drake tried to take my elbow to lead me away. I tugged it from him and placed both hands on the desk, lifting myself up as tall as I could go. "I want to know why this wasn't looked into." I cocked my head toward the symbol.

"Miss!" the older cop shouted. "If you would like to file a motion to open the case up again, by all means, go ahead." His lips pressed tight together before they opened again. "But until then, I suggest you leave. Now."

My blood pulsed in my head so hard I could feel my skin throbbing, like a needle dipping up and down, approaching warning temperatures. Drake's lips moved on my ear. "Come on, Sarah. I know this hurts. Let's get out of here and we'll talk about it."

My body deflated, conforming to Drake's soft arms. He nodded at Pauly and Rudy while he led me away. When I felt the crisp night air, I collapsed into him.

He held tight, arms encapsulating me. After a few minutes, I moved away, not caring my mascara probably left my eyes black-rimmed with trails of dark tears down my cheeks. His fingertips lightly brushed them out. "I'm sorry," I choked.

"Me too," he reassured. He cleaned me up, his thumb trailing my cheekbone. "Where else have you seen that symbol?"

I breathed in the cool air, allowing it to calm me. "At the Wiccan meeting." I nodded, remembering the eyes that blazed with the lightning symbol. "Remember I asked you about a symbol on our way home? When I freaked out. That was why. I saw that symbol." I started to rattle again, hands shaking.

"Shh," he soothed.

"Do you know what it is?" I asked, searching his face.

"No."

My shoulders sunk, deflated. "I'm sorry I accused your grandfather."

Drake shrugged. "That's just another reason you can't use not to date me."

I smirked and thought about kissing him, but remembered how he wanted more the last time. Drake would always want more. He wasn't like the use 'em and lose 'em type from Miami. The kind I used to lament about with friends. Now that I had a gentleman—a perfect gentleman who wanted me—I was scared. Who would want me when I'd probably end up being just like my mother anyway?

I sighed and laughed at the same time, my feelings as screwed up as my relationships. "No, I guess I can't use that as an excuse."

I ran my fingers through my hair and wiped at my face. "I need to find out what that symbol is."

I looked up at Drake, hoping for an answer.

He shrugged. "Google it?"

****

When I returned to Rose's, I turned my phone on immediately, ignoring the beeps as new text messages came in. The signal wasn't strong enough to get on the web through the phone, but I could try to connect to a wireless signal.

The phone beeped. *No Connection.*

"Ugh. I really *am* living in the 50's." I tossed the phone on the end table in the foyer. "Rose, are you here?" I called out. "You'll never guess where I've been." I searched the dark foyer. "I've been at the police station. I think something happened to my—"

"There you are," her aunt's voice bellowed. "You are not the only one in this house, you know." Rose pointed up the stairs. "I'm trying to sleep, but I can't with all that noise you're making up there."

"Noise?" I walked forward shaking my head. I told her where I was going. "I've been with Drake, I haven't—"

The older woman's eyes narrowed. A physical pulse of anger shockwaved her body. Rose's voice turned haughty, like an 1800's gentleman talking to a poor, ignorant servant. "If you weren't here, then why did I hear bangs coming from your room? I know you're upset about your father, but that is not the way to handle it."

"I have no idea what you've been hearing." My voice sounded small next to the authoritative tone of my aunt's.

"Did you have Drake over? Is that what you've been doing up in your room?" Rose's face turned to disgust.

"No!" I shouted, shocked she would insinuate anything like that. My cheeks burned in embarrassment.

"We weren't here…and I haven't been doing anything like…like—"

"And I am not a small town hick as you may think I am. I have enough senses to trust my ears when I hear things." Rose thrust her finger up the stairs. "You are the only one here besides me."

"Rose, really, I haven't been here. Come, check."

"I will check!" Rose's face enflamed, shaking with anger. I watched her implode, not understanding how the warm aunt I saw around Drake could flip like a switch and turn into Britney Spears with a shaved head and an umbrella.

Rose turned on the heel of her pink slippers and clopped up the stairs. I arched my eyebrows in amazement, remembering my father calling her 'spry' in the journal. I thudded up the stairs to catch up with her, reaching the top just as Rose turned the doorknob. She peeked at me and smiled with one lip curved up too much, making it look like a snarl.

I closed the gap between us in two strides. We both stood in the doorway now. I peeked in, making sure I didn't have underwear lying around or something else to make Rose think Drake and I were actually fooling around. The other investigated for who knew what. A clue in some phantom bangs case?

"The noises are coming from here," Rose said, walking to the corner of the room. A few steps in, her head snapped back, curlers jumping in an escape attempt, but they buoyed right back. "No wonder." The older woman pointed at the desk. "You've moved it!" The wrinkled hand gave way to long, perfectly polished red nails, no scratches or peeling. "Why did you move that desk?" Her teeth clenched.

"I have no idea what you're talking about. I didn't touch the desk." My pulse quickened, throbbing in my wrist first, then in my temples. Anger and apprehension swirled around inside in a tornado of mixed emotions. "The desk has been there since you told me to come up here that first night. Why would I bother to move furniture around?"

"That is impossible. I moved that desk to the attic years ago."

"I'm not sure what's going on here." I exhaled a deep breath. It whistled out like a steam-run train.

The rigidness of Rose's shoulders softened. She took a deep breath and let it out all in one whoosh. Her face was expressionless while she stared at me, though judging by her opaque eyes, not really seeing me. Fleeting though it was, I caught the look and then suddenly she was out of it.

Rose walked toward the desk, letting her fingers play over the wood. Closing her eyes and muttering, she talked in whispers, her voice low. There was a repetition to whatever she said, a melodic tune.

"What's wrong?" I took a few steps closer to the corner of the room. "Are you okay?"

Rose cocked her head. "It can't be," she choked out, face paling white. "It can't be." Suddenly, she ripped her hand away from the desk. Gaping down at her pointer finger, she gasped. The tip of her finger was red and bulging. "You brought it out! You brought it out!"

I started to tremble, uneasiness quivering through me. "Aunt Rose, I…"

The older woman came at me with careful, purposeful steps. When she was right in my face, she said, "No. You brought it out." She quickly turned and walked out the door, letting it slam behind her.

I reached in my pocket for my phone. I needed to talk to Drake. Maybe my dad was right. Rose didn't seem at all with it. She went through mood swings like crazy and she had to be way past the point of menopause symptoms. This was possibly menopause on steroids.

I patted my pocket. Not there. *Crap. I left it downstairs.* I bent over the desk, eyeing the wood design for any clues as to why Rose freaked. It just looked like a desk to me, an old one, but with the same drawers and cubbies like any other desk.

Hell, it looked a lot like the desk Mom bought me after engagement number one didn't work out.

Johnny Brimbauer. His wife had died, leaving him with no kids. I really liked him actually, even begged him to stay. Plotted out a route to run away, straight to Johnny's house on the water after they broke up. Come to think of it, my mother had bought me a whole new bedroom set for that one.

This time I ran away to true family. I wasn't doing it again.

I crossed the room to the door and eased it open, listening, reminding myself of the first night, except this time Rose was being crazy and not my mom. For once, not my mom.

Quick footsteps paced the wood floor below. My heart beat in time with them until I lost all nerve and retreated back to the room. The house phone rang before I could get there. The shrill ring screeched through the silent house, like the owl piercing the nighttime forest.

"Hello," Rose barked. I didn't need to descend the steps this time. My aunt's voice was loud enough to hear standing on the landing outside my room. "No. No. She's in bed already." The footsteps halted. "A symbol? No, she didn't tell me…" The older woman's voice softened. "Well, I imagine she is upset." I inched down the first couple steps. "David's journal? It's in the library. Why?" And after a moment of silence, "Oh, I see. Huh. Well, it's probably just some symbol that he liked." The footsteps started up again. They got louder as they neared the foyer, but they turned, sounding as if she moved toward the library door. At least in that vicinity. I hid in the hallway, out of view from the staircase. A big, throaty laugh echoed through the open room downstairs. "Yeah, she definitely is that, isn't she, Drake?" I bit down on my lip. The phone beeped after Rose said goodbye and something about the lawn mower.

Rose's footsteps continued on until the room fell silent. I only waited a minute before descending the stairs. I needed to get the journal back.

At the bottom step, I stood and listened. Off in the other room, a mattress groaned.

The journal was the key. Too bad it was in the library. *I'll just slip in, take it out, and have it back before she gets up in the morning*, I promised myself.

Tiptoeing across the floor, cringing when the floorboards groaned and creaked, I stopped and listened. Rose's room remained quiet. Only two more steps to the library and I'd be home free. One step…two steps…the board near the door sighed. I cringed again, ears straining to listen. Nothing.

The doorknob was cold and the metal rattled when I turned it. Well, tried to turn it.

"Sarah, is that you?"

I jumped and leapt back into the middle of the large room, eyes darting to the shadowy corners, searching for the voice. The lights flickered on. Rose emerged, one eye slightly closed as the light from the chandelier shone down on her. "Sorry. I was just looking for…" The R drew out as I scanned the room for something to save me. "My phone! I was searching for my phone," I said, spying it on the end table. "I couldn't remember where I put it."

I crossed to the table and picked the cell up, holding it out to show Rose. The old woman nodded. "Okay, honey. Get some sleep now." She rubbed my back as she guided me toward the stairs. "Drake said you had a bad day. We'll talk about it later though. A nice, long rest will do you good."

I nodded and managed to mumble a "Thanks." In actuality, a nice, long stay in a sane town would do me good.

What really worried me, though wasn't why Rose's mood had flipped again, it was why Dad's journal had been locked in the damn library.

ERIN BUTLER

Chapter Fourteen

1639

The rusted metal latch clinked into place as Isabella's mother secured the door behind Mr. Lynne's retreating steps. In her bedroom, Isabella's ears perked, listening for the sounds of her mother busying herself for bed. The light of the full moon washed over her while she sat at the desk, waiting. The traveling cloak Mrs. Lynne passed down was already tied around her neck, warming her insides despite nervous chills spiking her skin. Thomas had not come to her in weeks. She must see him.

From watching her father, Isabella learned he went witch-hunting every other night. The only piece of information she lacked? What night Thomas went out on. Happily, her father let it slip yesterday that Thomas Ludington led the party on the nights he did not go hunting. He griped that he got "Old Man Ludington, who could find a witch in a garden full of roses…"

As the first sounds of her mother's wheezing snore sounded from within the room next door, Isabella willed herself to stay seated. By the time her mother's usual deep groans reverberated, her fingertips ached from grasping the desk so firmly.

As easy as before, she slipped through the house and outside. Mrs. Lynne expected her daughter to be dutiful. She harbored no worries Isabella would try to see Thomas again.

A pang of guilt slowed her step, but as the road came into view, she ran toward the trees for cover. The night moved all around her. She heard not only her quick, light steps through the branch and leaf-toppled floor, but the scamper of small animals. Overhead, the groans from tree branches echoed as they succumbed to the weight of an owl or the pressure of the wind.

Halfway to town, a voice bellowed. It carried on the breeze until it smacked Isabella in the chest, sending her heart skipping. She sank low to the forest floor and hid her face behind the hood of the cloak. The earthen floor soaked the dress at her knees as she crawled behind the trunk of a huge oak tree. It smelled of fresh mud and bitter moss.

As the sounds of men talking drew close, she peeked around the tree. A group of twenty, some young enough that she bettered them in age, walked down the road with sticks that burned with fire. The orange flames licked at the moon. Mr. Ludington led them. A younger brother to Thomas held the fire high for the magistrate, sweeping it along the far side of the road. Both hunters gazed into the darkness of the forest with drawn-in, expectant faces.

Near the end of the pack, Isabella spied her own father. He held no torch or light and walked with his eyes to the road as if he expected a witch to appear there. Isabella remained still, as sturdy as the oak before her and breathed in shallow breaths to avoid sound. Only when the flames of the torches grew dim, and then dark, did she allow herself to move on.

As she neared Adams village, Isabella's expectations drained to the dank forest floor. A watchman stood guard at the point where the country road opened into town. Hope extinguished to a tiny burning flame of a candle. She would have to wait it out.

Wrapped in her traveling cloak, Isabella hid behind a pile of chopped wood. Her hiding spot left her with ample view of the guard as she willed him to fall asleep or tire of waiting and leave. Neither made any outward noises. The chirping of the grasshoppers' chorus invaded the still of the town. No light came from windows, nor smoke from chimneys. No persons moved about tasting the alleviation of drink. This is not what she knew town life to be like.

The cheeping of the grasshoppers ceased. Isabella stiffened as the air around her buzzed. The guard noticed too. His head turned from one side of the road to the other, searching the shadows. A crow's screech pierced the night sky as a hand pounded down on Isabella's shoulders. Startled, she kicked away, sending logs from the pile toppling to the hard ground.

Thomas' eyes bulged when he recognized her. Fast steps approached off to their right. He held up his hand. "'Tis me James," he called out. "I tripped over some wood while walking the outskirts." The young man hesitated. Isabella's cloak shrouded her in darkness. "I am well." James grunted and retreated to his post.

Thomas held out his hand and led Isabella further into the woods. Finally, he turned to her. "Why are you here?" he asked. The moonlight washed out his face.

"I needed to see you." Her legs unsteady, she felt as if she'd ridden a hundred miles on her father's workhorse.

She stepped toward him. Thomas immediately closed the distance, grasped her hands, and squeezed. "Oh, Isabella. How I've missed you." He traced invisible lines with his fingers. They stood still for a long moment, Isabella's eyes closed, wishing for it not to end.

The traces came to a stop. Isabella's eyes fluttered open and she stared at Thomas whose face sat much closer to her now. He lifted his hand and traced a line from Isabella's ear to her jaw. She swallowed, her mouth suddenly dry.

Thomas almost laughed. "Why are you here? You could have been seen."

Isabella stared at him, eyes focused on the lines that etched his face. She wanted to say that she did not care, but the words would not come.

Thomas looked at her in earnest, his finger still tracing the same line on her face, his thumb skimming her cheek. "You had the courage to do what I could not." His fingers ceased moving. "I am bound to you. My heart is yours, Isabella."

She stood mute. Tears gathered at the corners of her eyes. The enormity of her actions squeezed her chest.

"Father has me leading hunts and preparing trials." Isabella's chin dropped. Thomas took her face in both his hands, cupping her behind the head. The tie in her hair came loose and her hair swirled around his fingers. "You have the loveliest green eyes. How I've missed those eyes." He bent down, slightly pulling on his hands. She reached up and grabbed his arm. The muscle rippled underneath as he tightened from her touch. She traced the indent of his skin.

Isabella leaned in, grazing her cheek with his. Her hair stood up on the back of her neck as his hot breath blew on her ear. "I do not need a ceremony, nor permission to feel this way." Thomas' shoulders sunk and he fell into her. They embraced in one another's arms. He stroked her hair all the way down to the small of her back.

She felt his heart beat as she moved her hands to his chest. The rise and fall of his body next to her made her feel safe. She laid her head on his shoulder and closed her eyes again, imagining doing this every night.

He finally moved, put his hands on her shoulders and pushed her away. One of the corners of his mouth pulled higher than the other. His eyes twinkled in the moonlight and his hair stood on end, not orderly as usual.

"Isabella," Thomas breathed, moving his hands to the back of her head again. The tips of his fingers only spaces apart. "I will talk to my father about us."

Isabella found her voice; it came out in a rasp. "My mother knows, Thomas." His eyes widened. "Mrs. Shipton has told her."

"How does she know?"

"She spied us."

His face swelled. "She is evil. I am determined to sway my father and—"

"My mother thinks I am a fool." Tears leaked from her eyes, leaving a stream of salty water down her cheeks. "She does not believe you care for me."

"I *shall* speak to him!"

His voice echoed around the trees. The forest quieted again.

Isabella opened her mouth to speak, but a thrash of footsteps disturbed the dry leaves. Thomas dropped his hands and hid Isabella behind him.

They heard the sound again, this time along with breaking twigs and leaves mashing one right after another until Magistrate Ludington stood before them, horse breaths snorting out his mouth and nose.

ERIN BUTLER

Chapter Fifteen

Present Day

The stairs of the old Victorian curved around at the bottom into the vestibule where Rose and I had met for the first time. I stood there the next afternoon, fingers tapping the wood of the banister, waiting for Drake to show. I'd checked my cell phone twice already for the time before the front door opened and Drake appeared. "Sorry I'm late," he said.

"It's okay." I shrugged and led him into the dining room to grab the snacks Rose prepared.

After Rose found me hiding in my room earlier, she scolded me for not telling her about the police station. I was too shocked and discombobulated to argue with her. Then, she insisted I invite Drake over and immediately busied herself in the kitchen, making cookies and cake. If I didn't know any better, I'd think Rose was a cougar.

She knew all his favorites, listing them off one-by-one, making sure she had all the ingredients to make two of his ultimate, all-time favorites. She put the radio on and started whistling and humming, which wasn't so bad, but then she started murmuring how Drake liked extra chocolate chips and poured almost two bags in. It was at that point I decided to wait somewhere else. You'd thought she had the date with him, not me.

"Ooh, my favorite." Drake grabbed a handful of chocolate chip cookies and then followed me as I ran up the stairs to my room. "Mmm, extra chips," he garbled around a mouthful.

I rolled my eyes. "Here it is. The infamous desk." I gestured to the corner.

Drake walked over and reached out to it. "So, this is the one she freaked out about?"

"Yep. What do you think?"

"No idea. Looks like a desk."

"Do you think your grandpa would know?"

"I told you, Sarah. I don't want my grandfather involved in this. He's old. He's sick. He doesn't need to worry about anything. Especially if it's just that Rose is having an issue with you staying with her."

"Drake. You should have seen her. She went completely insane. Screaming and pointing at me like I was some kind of intruder."

"Has she mentioned it again?"

"No. She was actually kind of nice this morning…and last night. Mostly after you agreed to come over."

Drake sat down and patted the bed. "What exactly did she say?"

I sighed, trying not to let my anger show. I already replayed the scene for him several times. "She told me I let *it* out. Whatever *it* is."

He grabbed my hands and pulled me on top of him. Our faces inches apart. Our bodies smooshed together, perfectly lined up. "And the symbol?"

I swallowed a catch in my breath. "I didn't have a chance to ask her about it." I barely recognized my own voice, it sounded breathy and soft.

A tiny smile tugged at Drake's lips. I wondered if he felt how fast my heart beat through his thin shirt. He laced his fingers through mine. "Did you check anywhere else?"

"When are you going to stop asking questions and help me figure out what the hell is going on here?" I wanted to sound angry. I wasn't sure I was convincing though. I wasn't sure it was possible to be mad at someone when I kept staring at their lips and all I wanted to do was smother his mouth with mine.

"Hey-hey-hey, Sarah. Calm down." He tucked a piece of hair behind my ear that had fallen loose, dangling between us.

"Sorry," I managed to mutter.

"Everything's going to be just fine. I'm sure Rose had a good reason. You probably spooked her too."

I rolled my eyes.

Drake threw me over onto the bed, flipping us like a pancake. He hovered above me now. "Stop rolling your eyes at me princess."

"Or what?" I giggled.

"I won't ever kiss you."

My mouth opened, then shut again. Could he tell that was all I thought about? He should be the psychic instead of these Crazies. "What makes you think I want you to kiss me?"

"Please. It's written all over you." I tried to flip him and failed. He lowered his body onto mine until I barely breathed. "You keep looking at me like I'm something to eat. I mean, I'm flattered, but—"

"But we have more important things to worry about right now?"

The teasing smile dropped from his face. My heart fluttered around in my chest, suspended in midair without a clue of which way to go next. He pushed himself up and gave me his hand to help me. "Let's do some research down in her library."

"You can't be serious." The side of my lip curled. "She told me to stay out of that room."

"It'll be fine.

"It was locked yesterday."

"Do you have a bobby pin?" Drake asked. I crossed to the bathroom and came out with one, handing it over. "Excellent."

"Are you seriously going to pick the lock?" Drake turned on his heels and left the room.

Giggling, I followed Drake down the stairs. He seemed taller to me, cuter even, if that was possible. Hey, he was willing to break a rule for me.

"Have you ever been in here before?" I whispered as Drake finally got the door unlocked.

"Once. With my dad," he returned in a casual voice.

"Why aren't you whispering?"

"Why are you?"

"I've got a better question," another voice severed the light-hearted banter. "Why are you both in here?"

Drake recovered before me and seemed fine. His shock turned into that charming look he gave when he wanted to be cute. "Hi, Rose. We were looking for you actually." I didn't start at the lie. It sounded like a good cover-up.

"Why is that?" Her voice strained, caught somewhere between nice and pissed.

Drake always worked magic on her though. "Sarah was upset about the conversation you had last night and wanted to know why the desk upset you."

Totally not what I even remotely said. Of course, mentioning I believed Rose went nuts last night probably wouldn't help us at this point.

Rose sneered at me as she took the question in. "She broke into the attic and brought down the desk, Drake." Rose's voice was softer now, more pleasant. I clamped my mouth shut before I spouted off something not so nice.

Drake made a noise with his throat. Probably a warning. "Regardless of how it got there…" Drake waved the accusation away. "What is it about the desk that makes you so upset?"

"I'm sure you've heard the story. Don't you remember?"

Drake shook his head. "I remember something about a desk. A story my dad told me, maybe, but I can't remember any specifics."

"Hmm. Interesting. I'm sure you will one day."

"You're not going to tell me?" His eyebrows went up in the center, like it pained him that she wouldn't tell him.

"Why? I know you'll remember." Rose smiled. "It's just that it's a family heirloom. Very old."

"Whose family?"

"One of the first settlers. I don't remember which right now."

"Can I use your library to look it up?"

"No. And definitely not with her." She stared me down. It was so weird. Every time it was just the two of them talking, Rose was an angel, the patron saint of niceties. Whenever I got mentioned, or spoke, she flipped her lid. Wasn't I supposed to be family?

"Okay, Rose. We'll just have to do research somewhere else." He shrugged and grabbed my hand. "Thanks anyway."

I could barely wait until we were in my room before saying, "*Thanks anyway?* Are you serious?"

"What? If I was rude to her, she'll never tell us anything again."

"She'll never tell *us* anything anyways. Maybe you."

He took both my hands and held them in front of him. "Would it be so bad if I get it out of her and then told you?"

"You probably won't have to, *I know you'll remember*," I said mockingly.

"You're right. I probably will." Drake's smile crinkled his eyes and revealed the tiny lines around his mouth.

"This isn't some joke." I squeezed his hands. "I'm really upset about all this. Why won't she tell *me*? I'm her niece."

"Come here." He tapped the quilt as he sat on the bed and I followed him, tucking my legs underneath me. "I know it's not a joke. I'm positive that Rose is just having a hard time accepting you right now. She's dealing with a lot of things too. I'm sure she put your father out of her head, now you being here is dragging it all up again. Those books in that library mean a lot to her. They hold the history of this town."

But I'm a person, family, not some stupid book. "She acted so crazy last night. I thought she might hurt me."

"Rose could never hurt anybody, let alone, you."

"What about the desk?"

"I'm positive the desk won't hurt you either."

"Drake. Be serious."

"I am. The desk, even if there is some creepy story about that particular desk, which is stretching it for sure, it's all just legend. So Rose gets spooked about a ghost story. That doesn't mean you need to be. Come on." Drake locked his eyes on mine and raised his eyebrows. "I think I know what you need."

"What's that?"

"You need time not talking about weird symbols, worrying about weird symbols, and researching weird symbols. Let's do something fun. Total normal teenager fun."

****

Drake's idea of total normal teenager fun involved a bonfire in the woods. And a party. I could go for a party.

I let Drake drive the Escalade. We drove down the same dirt road for the Wiccan meeting. This time, instead of candles and prayers, the Crazies tried to vibrate two-hundred year old trees with loud, thumping music and light up the sky with a blazing fire. The burning wood sent thick smoke into the dusk night, clearly visible from back on the main road. "You guys don't get in trouble?"

"Nah. The cops leave us alone during the festival. They have too much other stuff to worry about." He peeked at me briefly, hands still holding on to the steering wheel firmly at ten and two. I threatened him with his life. "Of course if they hear you're here, they'll probably make a special trip."

I laughed. "Do you think your cop friend thinks I'm a nut job?"

"Probably, but I'm sure he sees a lot of 'em."

I smirked at Drake. He wore a pair of nice jeans with a loose fitting polo, hair gelled and spiked. "So, did you dress up for your old girlfriends?"

"Ha. No…"

I peered down at myself, noticing we somehow exchanged fashions. I wore a plain white v-neck over blue jeans and sneakers, liking the fact I didn't have to wear heels every time I went out. "You look nice," I told him.

"Nice, huh?" He nodded his head and shrugged. "I'll take nice."

Groups stood near coolers and passed around drinks. Some swayed back and forth to music, and more than a few made out along the fringes where the firelight barely reached.

Now this reminded me of home. Except for the forest part. Sneaking out to beach parties was more my scene back home. Who knew, forest parties could be fun too.

"What do you want to drink?" Drake asked, hopping out of the SUV.

"What do you got?"

Drake led me over to a cooler. He said hey to a few friends as they parted, leaving us a straight shot to raid the drinks.

Beer. And a lot of it.

"I didn't know you rolled like this," I joked.

Drake smiled. "Which kind?"

"The bottle." Drake opened it for me and I took a sip, face puckering. I'd much rather have a fruity daiquiri or wine.

The heat of the fire drew me closer. I used to camp with Jamie and her family until we grew out of it at about the age of thirteen or so. About the age where we wanted to look at lifeguards more than we wanted to eat 'Smores. Thirteen—the age where you questioned everything. The age I realized my mother was a joke.

"What are you smirking at?"

I looked over at Drake. His face reflected the orange flames. "My mother."

"What about her?"

I shook my head and laughed. "I was just thinking how when I was thirteen, it started to really bother me that Mom would bring home her 'guy friends'." I picked up a branch and stuck the end in the fire. "She wanted me to become friends with all these guys, yet she wouldn't tell me anything about my own father. She wanted me to know that John Smith had a condo in the Hamptons, but didn't even want to tell me what team my father liked in baseball. She wanted me to care about these other, stupid guys."

I brought the flaming stick to my mouth and blew it out, leaving the tip burning like hot coal. "One fight in particular, she told me she 'threw all his shit away' because all it did was piss her off to look at it." I wrote my name in cursive in the sky, tiny embers flying off the edge of the stick, leaving a trail of orange glow as I swooped the letters. "Well, now that pissed *me* off. She took away my ability to find out about my own father because of what it did to her." I turned the S into a D and started writing Dad's name in the cursive that resembled his, over and over until the sparks died. "That's my selfish mother for you."

I threw the stick in the fire and downed the rest of the beer. It went down easier than taking little sips. Drake put his arm around me and squeezed. I lifted my chin and stared at him. His eyes mirrored the flames before he closed them and moved closer. I let him, meeting him in the middle.

My kiss was eager, more romantic than friendship like the last time we kissed. I kissed him like I wanted to earlier when we laid on my bed. When our hearts beat together. When his lips looked so soft. They were soft.

"You know I really like you," Drake said. "It sounds to me like you shouldn't even go back to Florida."

He talked out his ass. "What? Am I just supposed to stay here?"

He shrugged. "Even if you did go back. It's not like you and I don't have cell phones, or computers. And I don't know if you've heard, they have this new invention called an airplane. It could really be useful—"

"Shut up."

I reached up on my toes to kiss him again, but he stopped me. "I'm serious."

"I know." I put my fingers around his neck and pulled him to me, kissing him again before turning back to the blaze.

He took my bottle from me. "You want another one?"

"Sure."

He left me staring at the fire. The front of my face melted, sweat popping up on my temples. I turned to warm by backside and noticed Marlene walking toward me. *Fan-freakin-tastic. I hope we get into a fight about Drake. That would just make my day.*

"Hey." Marlene's head nodded up and down like a bobblehead. "Saw you kiss Drake over here."

Oh yeah, so much fun. "Yup," I popped the p. Why did girls do this? *He broke up with you. Get it?*

"I wanted to let you know that when you go back home, I'll be the one here."

I smiled. "And that's supposed to bother me..." Marlene cocked her eyebrow.

I didn't want to fight. Yes, I'd have to leave someday. Of course I wanted to tell her to mind her own freaking business, but what would that solve?

Marlene shrugged and went to turn away. The flames caught on the silver necklace and the glare sparked my attention. "Hey Marlene, where'd you get that necklace?"

Marlene twisted around, scowling. "Rose gave it to me."

"Rose?" My tummy did a funny flip. Rose gave her presents? Why? It wasn't like she really was Drake's grandma. They weren't even related.

"Oh. Yeah." She smirked. "When Drake and I were dating." She picked up the circle in her fingers and rubbed her thumb over the smooth surface, looking down at the shine she gave it. "She said I was Drake's now and that I should have this."

"What is it?"

"Who knows? I don't even really care. I just thought the symbol was cool. See." Marlene held it out for me, the chain pulling taut around her neck. "It looks like a lightning bolt in the middle."

I nodded. Yeah, I had seen alright. Too many times before.

"Oh, do I detect jealousy?" Marlene frowned. "Ya know, that's really not an attractive quality. I know Drake doesn't like it."

This chick was ridiculous. "Whatever."

"I did. I got to you, didn't I?" Marlene laughed. "As soon as you're gone, Drake and I are getting back together." I stopped moving, but didn't say anything. "We're meant for each other. We can't help it."

I whirled. "Who told you that, your fairy godmother?"

"Aww, look how your face gets all red when you're mad. How cute." Marlene giggled into her hands.

"Just…save it bitch. I don't—"

Marlene waltzed right up to me and leaned down. The foul bite of fermented leftovers stained the air between us as she whispered in my face, "No. Rose told me. We're to be together. We're meant to be together." I took a few steps back. Meant to be together? Marlene looked around and then yelled, "You think you're big shit, don't you?" Faces turned to stare at us. "You think you're just some city girl that can come traipsing in here and mess everything up. Well, you can't."

"What are you talking about?" Faces crowded in around us.

"Drake's mine. Everybody here knows he's mine. So just leave!" Everyone started to nod, like Marlene gave some moving sermon they all agreed with.

I stood speechless. A fire from a gas stove cooked in me, heating my blood. "You're crazy, you know that? If you've got a problem with Drake and I, tell Drake. From what I can tell, he's not into you anymore."

Marlene's nostrils flared, reminding me of a horse on a cold morning. I half expected fog to start shooting out. The crowd moved in closer and I smelled the intoxicating, sour beer on all of them. *Where the hell is Drake?* "Well, he is mine. He is." Marlene fingered the pendant on her necklace again.

I shook my head and turned my back on Marlene. I moved through the crowd and they parted for me, leaving a line about four people deep to parade in front of. Everyone shot me dirty looks or looked away disgusted. Even Drake's friend Pete, who the other day couldn't believe how lucky Drake was, practically spit on my feet. *Jesus, do they stick by their own or what?*

As I broke through the mob, Drake came trudging out of the woods. "Where the hell were you?" I asked.

"I had to pee." He motioned to the trees. "Why?"

"Marlene." I rolled my eyes and hugged myself. "Your friends almost went all lynch mob on me."

"Huh?"

"Marlene. She just called me out in front of everybody. She said you were hers and to leave you alone." Drake reached out, but I stood back. I didn't need a stoning today.

"Sarah, nothing's going on—"

"What's up buddy?" Pete came over and slapped Drake on the back. He nodded toward me and said, "Hey, how's it goin'?"

I started. "Are you serious?"

"Yeah. What's up? You like it in town or what?" Pete plastered a smile on his face, his dark hair framing his features. Even his eyes looked genuine. His smile faded. "Oh hey, are we in a lover's quarrel already?" he joked. "Do you guys need some alone time or something?"

I just stared at him, so Drake said, "Nah man, we're good. Sarah was sayin' Marlene gave her a hard time."

"She did? When? Man, I told you that girl was trouble. Just because Rose said you should go out with her, didn't mean you had to."

Drake drew his eyes in, then looked back and forth between Pete and me, so I planted a fake smile on my face and rested my hands on my hips. "Did you get me something else to drink or what?"

****

Drake shot me weird looks throughout the night. The entire night. His friends, everybody, didn't let him get close to me the rest of the party. They swarmed around, eager to talk about anything besides Adams.

Every time a new person approached—and they were mostly guys; must have been slim pickings in Adams—I searched the faces for Drake. Every time, I found him shaking his head. *He's probably wondering what the hell kind of crazy girl he's got himself mixed up with.*

A six-foot tall jock stood in front of me now. Yapping. I noticed his mouth move, but wasn't interested in anything that came out of it.

"Hey…" I interjected, "sorry to cut you off…um…"

"Josh." The jock flexed his muscles and showed off his sloppy grin.

"Josh." I smiled back at him. "But listen, I'm um…" *Not interested.* "…not feeling good. I think I need to find Drake so he can drive me home."

"If you want, I can take you."

I shook my head. "Thanks, but we drove my car."

"The Escalade, right?" The jock twitched his face, flicking hair out of his eyes. "That car is sick. I'll drive you home in it if you want. I only live like two miles away from Rose." That was enough of that. I turned and fled.. "I can walk home," he called out as I walked away.

I finally found Drake near the fire in what appeared to be a heated conversation with Marlene. I stepped toward them as he threw a water bottle into the flames. Marlene's cheeks were damp, the orange glow of the fire mirrored on her skin.

I stopped, deciding to give them some time. Maybe he did believe me and was telling her off. It would be nice to have someone believe me. Besides, I needed to pee anyway. The forest where Drake reappeared earlier loomed in front of me. I shrugged and trudged in. *Hey, there's a first time for everything.*

By the time I got to a space that even remotely resembled a nice place to squat, my head throbbed. I did my business by a small stream, then moved a little way down and found a log to sit on. I laid my head on my knees and closed my eyes, concentrating on the sound of the running water and the hoot of the owls, trying to completely forget everything that had been happening.

I breathed deep, in through the nose and out the mouth to calm the electric nerves that sizzled and sparked. They were fading now, with every breath I took, I was fading, until I was lost in my own mind.

I was a blank page, wishing I could start this story over again. Maybe I wouldn't have ended in Adams, at my aunt's house, at the bank of the stream where I couldn't find the energy to muster any physical response when it happened.

A figure.

Standing at the edge of the tree line, chapped lips smirking and holding a bundle of smoking straw, a figure engulfed in shadows and moonlight walked toward the bank of the creek. Embers fizzled out as the shadow blew on the swathed talisman. A gray cloud curled up, surrounding the sallow face and floating upward. The dark veil descended on me. Fire marinated the hay, producing an earthy smell of freshly mowed grass and wood smoke that swallowed me up.

I was already gone, driven to the recesses of my mind, unaware of the outside forces at work.

ERIN BUTLER

Chapter Sixteen

1639

"To the house now, both of you. I will speak to you there."

"Sir…" Thomas started.

"Now!" Branches snapped all around as quick feet barreled through the woods toward them.

Thomas took Isabella's hand and ran to the house. Her chest squeezed tight, her breaths labored as she had to dig deep to gulp in air. "This way," he said, tugging her around a corner of another house before they reached his. He crashed through the front door, sending it thudding against the wall.

Mrs. Ludington ran into the hallway and then stopped in her tracks. "Isabella Lynne?" She looked at her son. "What is she doing here?"

Thomas dropped Isabella's hand. Her heart sank with it as it fell to her side. "Mother…I…"

Heavy footsteps carried into the entryway. Isabella turned and took a step behind Thomas as Mr. Ludington banged the door shut. "Go to your room, Martha. I need to speak with our son."

She nodded her head, obliging him and walked with her head up, back to the other room. "Sir—" Thomas started again, but he was interrupted.

"Thomas, would you like to tell me why you were meeting in the woods with this…girl?" he shot out.

"I—"

"And why, during these times, you left your post? You left another guard to become bewitched? Is this how you show your gentlemanly honor to our village?" His father strode up next to him and Isabella mirrored the movement, taking a few steps back.

Thomas stood tall. "I was walking my rounds when I happened across Isa—Miss Lynne."

The older man's eyebrow peaked. Then he turned to Isabella, "And what excuse do you have for being in the woods at night?"

His dark eyes bore into her and a single bead of sweat rolled down her back. "Sir, I—"

"She came to see *me*, Father."

Mr. Ludington looked from one to the other. "What are you speaking of, Thomas?"

"Miss Lynne and I are in love. I wish to marry her."

****

Isabella sat at her desk that night, hoping to hear a tap at the window. She still believed in Thomas, in them as a couple. He and Magistrate Ludington escorted her home earlier under the guise of a witch hunter. Thomas' eyes appeared hopeful. His father's were dark. Though the judge said he would think on the matter, she dared not hope too much. His silence revealed everything to her. He vowed he would not tell anyone of her suspicious appearance in town. Isabella, however, knew he did that only for his son, even when it garnered an encouraging smile from Thomas.

Isabella exhaled loudly. She placed her quill on the desk. No more words came. Her heart did not wish to write this letter to Thomas. It could break him…them.

Isabella slid back from the desk. It glowed yellow, sometimes orange. Strange, she felt as if someone's eyes watched her. Glared at her. A shiver ran up her spine. She ran her hands over the wood and closed her eyes, calming her nerves. With everything happening, she felt as if her insides were split in two. Her head told her one thing, while her heart screamed another.

The crickets chirped outside and the wind rushed through the trees and pushed against the house's exterior walls. It seemed to pick up speed and become louder as she sat there, eyes closed.

She gripped the hard, cold wood of the desk and squeezed her eyes tighter. So tight that swirls of white light sprang up from all corners. Her body coursed with shivering goosebumps and the hairs pricked on her arms.

Her stomach turned, panic rose through her as her heart beat out of control. She felt something. Something evil within the fringes of her body.

A voice sounded in her head. Impossible. It wasn't her own voice she was so used to hearing lately. It was foreign. It didn't belong, but it was also familiar. Out of place speaking in her own mind, though she knew who spoke.

Why?

Laughter rose up in her, yet it was not hers. It stayed there, lodged in her own thoughts that were not her own. It laughed and laughed.

Isabella tried desperately to open her eyes. The foreigner would not let her. Images flooded her mind. No conjuring of her own imagination and not memories, but bits and pieces seen through someone else.

ERIN BUTLER

Chapter Seventeen

Present Day

My body was in a weird state between being asleep and dreaming and being awake and dreaming. The numbness faded. Awareness crept back to me in inches.

As full realization returned, I stiffened. I wasn't where I thought I should have been. In the haziness between sleep and wakefulness, I had lost myself.

I was supposed to be by the bank of the stream. I felt next to my laying body, expecting soft dirt or mud. Instead, I felt the smooth folds of cotton. I moved my hands down toward my waist and still felt more cotton.

Is it possible that I woke up and drove back to Rose's and don't remember? Or even better, Drake drove me and I don't remember. Regardless, everything ends with me not remembering. I blinked away the sleepiness, rubbed my eyes and peered to the right, expecting to see the desk. That odd, beautiful desk.

My eyes finally cleared and I opened my mouth to scream. Nothing came out. I wasn't by the stream and I wasn't at Aunt Rose's. *Where the hell am I?* I peeked down at myself. I still wore the clothes I put on for the party, which was good. An unfamiliar patchwork quilt lay on top of me, orange and greens.

I was in a good-sized room, much like the room at my aunt's with old and out-of-date furniture. Paintings of country scenes surrounded me, roosters and chickens, barns and fences. Two windows streamed in light from behind, each on either side of the bed. I didn't know what time it was and a quick search of the room revealed no clock. *How long have I been sleeping? Was I sleeping?* It felt like sleep, but I usually slept light. *How did I get here?*

Footsteps creaked the floor. My hands automatically clenched into a fist around the quilt and I drew the blanket up around me. My mind returned to that too interested jock. Had he brought me here? Kidnapped me?

I thought about faking sleep, but figured if attacked, I wanted to have the advantage of being able to see what came after me. My heart raced, palms growing sweaty.

The footsteps moved closer, sounding like the clop, clop of a single person coming up a flight of stairs. My whole body tightened as a shadow moved underneath the door. A light shined in from below and someone stepped in front of the glow. My eyes grew to big discs on my face and I hugged my knees into myself. The click of the door handle sounded. I bit down on my cheeks, to stop myself from screaming.

And waited.

The door inched open. With each moment, I moved farther and farther up the bed, closer to the headboard. The door, finally fully open, allowed light to pour in and I had to blink away the sudden searing in my eyes. The shadow completely put out the light and my eyes gradually came into focus.

I breathed a big sigh. It was Drake.

"Hey Drunkard." He laughed. "A couple of my friends found you near the creek. They had to carry you to the car." He grabbed my hand. "So what the hell happened? One minute you were the talk of the town, guys were lined up to talk to you, and the next, you were gone."

"I thought I was sleeping." I looked up at him cautiously. *How did this happen? Did I faint? Why would I have fainted?*

"I don't think so, Sarah. Everyone tried to wake you up. You wouldn't."

"I don't think I ever fainted before," I said, a tug in my stomach. "I guess I don't know what happened."

"Sarah." Drake laughed again. "You passed out." He nodded his head when I shook mine. "Don't worry," he said, rubbing my shoulder. "It happens to the best of us. Rose doesn't know a thing. I called and told her you were too tired to drive home last night." His face smirked, but apprehension tugged at his eyes. "I was just really worried, up until we found you."

I smiled, trying to relieve the boiling pit in my stomach. "Why? Is crime rate high here?" The laughter that came from him soothed me, crept into my bones and massaged out the kinks.

He turned solemn after staring a while. "Don't get too freaked out okay?"

"Freaked out?" There was something more than not remembering what the hell happened to me last night?

"There's something you need to see."

He tugged on my hands, standing close beside me as he pulled me up and out of bed. All the blood rushed to my brain and tiny stars sparkled in and out before my eyes. I took a few steps and they disappeared. "What are we doing?"

"Here," he said, motioning to the dresser with the mirror. "Look. Pete and the guys said it was there when they found you."

"Pete found me?" I stepped in front of the mirror and gasped. It was worse than the Bloody Mary game I used to play as a kid. I reached up to my forehead and smudged a part of the circle. The circle encased a lightning bolt. "Oh. My. God." I looked down at my finger—black ash. "What is going on here?" My voice trembled so bad I barely spat out anything.

"Probably just people messing with you. Marlene maybe."

"Drake, you do know what this is, don't you?" I turned and pointed at my forehead.

"Yes. It's the symbol you keep seeing."

"It's the symbol that was found on my dad's dead body!"

"Sarah. He had a heart attack."

"Maybe. Why the symbol? And why now? On me?" I stared back at my reflection. "Why me?"

"Calm down. Someone's playing a joke on you."

"A joke. Seriously? No. This is not a joke. Who else even knows besides you and me about the symbol they found, huh? Who else?"

"I don't know."

He tried to grab for me, but I took a step closer to the door. "Me either. But somebody does. Somebody. Somebody is trying hard to scare me."

"What for?"

"I don't know. But I'm thinking my dad's death wasn't an accident." I took another step toward the door. "I'm going to request they open the case back up. I'm going to show them this…this symbol on me." I walked to the doorway and stopped. "But first. First, I'm going to talk to your grandfather."

"Sarah—"

"No Drake. You're not stopping me this time."

"Yes. I am." Drake moved in front of me, guarding me from the door. "I told you he's sick."

"He knows something about this."

"How do you know?"

I ran my fingers through my hair and tugged it down. "He has to."

"He ran over a man that happened to be dead already with a symbol on him. How would he know anything about it? Sarah! Your dad died of a heart attack, okay? I know you think you're doing something good by trying to figure out some sort of mystery surrounding his death, but there just isn't one. He's dead. He died of natural causes. Not some mysterious...god, I don't even know what the hell you think." Drake tossed his hands in the air. "You're not going to talk to Grandpa about it. He's all I have."

"At least you have someone." Tears slipped from my eyes and trickled down my face leaving wet tracks. I pushed past Drake and ran down the stairs. They led to the big oak front door I recognized from the other night. I ran through and slammed it behind me.

My black Escalade loomed in front of me in the driveway and I found the keys in the ignition. I rolled my eyes. *Stupid hick. Doesn't he know people steal cars? Especially nice cars, like this.*

I peeled off toward the police station and when I went in, I stood calmly as they took photos of my head, my eyes still stinging. My face blank, immovable, unchangeable, like gravity. It couldn't be disproved now. I didn't care what Drake said. Something was wrong.

The guy thanked me for coming in. He was not one of the two I freaked out in front of the other day. Thankfully. "The bathroom's over there if you want to freshen up."

I nodded. In the bathroom, I searched myself in the mirror one last time.

Branded.

Branded for what? By whom? I didn't know. Somebody thought they could mess with me though. I felt like a cow with one of those plastic earrings that said who they belonged to. My sooty forehead marked me as someone's. Now I needed to find out who thought they owned me.

I splashed water on my face and the mark easily came off, black smears cascading down the sink and into the drain. I kept scrubbing. I still felt like it was there, like the symbol held onto me. When I finally finished, the ash left dark smudges in the sink and I gave myself a pink, blotchy forehead to match my pink, blotchy eyes.

I stopped halfway through the bathroom threshold, the friendly cop's voice drifted over to me. "Don't you think we oughtta ask—?"

"Who? Courtney James?" Another officer stood partially hidden by shelves.

The nice cop turned my way. I drew back into the shadows. "Yeah."

"Why?" the other asked, acting as if the nice policeman was stupid.

"It looks like a Wiccan symbol to me."

"Please. It's kids playing jokes on each other. We don't have time for their crap with the festival going on. File it away."

My heart kickstarted. These people thought they were so smart. *I guess it's up to me. First step: Find Courtney James, High Priestess of the local coven.*

Chapter Eighteen

1639

Again, Isabella sought the warmth. The cold encased her, leaving her shrouded as if she sank deep into the frozen earth. The fire licked out again, calling her. Her pace quickened. As she was about to step through the clearing, the voice drifted to her. In melody, the woman sang,

> *Do you think it wise,*
> *child of your heart?*
> *They can see you with their eyes,*
> *you will soon part.*
> *And not together they will take you.*
> *They despise like the plague*
> *and you will wonder, but he scorns you,*
> *no matter his conscience to beg.*

Mother Shipton turned. Isabella knew it was her before she saw the long nose and the dark slats for eyes. The woman walked forward and did not hesitate at the fire. She walked through it, the flames bowing out around her, not catching at her clothes, and came through on the other side just how she looked before, a smile playing on her lips. "I do not burn, but you will."

Isabella's whole body shook, her shoulders heaved forward and backward until soon the movement roused her.

Thomas stood over her in bed. The breeze from the open window blasted her face, her sweat cooled as it dried on her head, arms, and neck. "Wake, Isabella. We must go."

"Mrs. Shipton?"

"No. Isabella, we have to go. Now." He flipped her sheets down.

"Go? Go where?"

"My father has forsaken me. He will not grant us our marriage."

"He said—"

"It does not matter what he said. It only matters what he says now. Come! Grab as few belongings as possible. I have got my best horse and we will leave this place."

"Leave my family? My home?"

"'Tis the only way we can be together."

"My father will talk to him." Isabella clutched her bed sheets. "I am sure he can be appealed to."

"My father will have none of it. He thinks I have made a bad choice in you."

Isabella stared through tear-glistened eyes. "Have I done something to offend him?"

"'Tis only your lack of wealth that offends him. Now grab as little as possible."

"But how will we live?" *And you will wonder, but he scorns you.*

"Does it matter?" Thomas took up her hand and forced it around his body. He bent over and kissed her, with all the excitement and hurry moving from his lips to hers. He pulled at her waist and she gathered the folds of his shirt at his back in her hands. He pulled away a little, their foreheads touching. "We will have one another. Now make haste!"

He spurred her to move. She threw the blankets off and moved about the room. She went first to the desk for her journal and then to the floorboards for Thomas' letters and placed them inside the leather book. Thomas opened his sack and Isabella tossed them inside. She grabbed a smock and petticoat and put it on over her nightgown and then placed another set in Thomas' bag. Finished, she looked at Thomas, her eyes wide. "Where are we to go?"

"To my uncle's first, before my father realizes I have gone. Then we will leave, find a place to live as husband and wife." He kissed her again and went to the window. Thomas threw the sack out first and then followed it before reaching back for Isabella.

The door to her room thudded open on its hinges. Her mother stood there, mouth hung open at the sight before her. Fear riddled her eyes. "Mother—?"

"They have come," she shouted. She looked down to Thomas who still held out his hands for Isabella. "To the barn."

"Mother?"

Mrs. Lynne came forward and grasped her daughter's hands. "Now."

"I have a horse. It will be faster."

Mrs. Lynne nodded.

Isabella turned and Thomas pulled her through the window. "We love you, Child," her mother said before her scream interrupted the hushed bedroom.

Isabella looked back to see her mother falling to the floor, tackled by Mr. Austen. She writhed, her legs kicking out, but he clasped her steady.

Thomas lifted Isabella from the window before they were spied and toward his horse. After a few steps, he halted. Isabella ran into him from behind, her gaze still lost in her mother's fight.

Isabella whirled around and once again, her fearful eyes lay upon Mr. Ludington.

ERIN BUTLER

Chapter Nineteen

Present Day

The horn beeped when I locked the SUV after cornering into a tiny parking space by the statue of the first settler. I glanced up at the tall, gray stone. It was a common landmark in the small towns where I stopped to rest on my way to Virginia, usually in off the highway exits. Most of those were military statues marked with old soldiers in uniforms holding rifles. This was a guy in trousers and a work shirt, a regular person settling this piece of new land. *Maybe he wanted a fresh start. Maybe he came to make a living to win a girl. Maybe*, I thought, staring up from this little piece of grass, *he wanted to make his father proud.*

His eyes were creepy, haunted. Unlike the other statues, which stared off at nothing, too high to be staring at any one person, this one's eyes followed you. I walked to the end of the grassy area, still keeping my eyes on him, and he watched me too. The entire way.

I turned around and stood right in front of him. Yup. He looked at me still. Way disturbing. An engraving on the statue bolded his last name—C. C something. The rest was gutted out, like someone had picked away at it. I searched around the base for a big fallen chunk. There wasn't one. On the opposite side, face down in the grass, I found a white paper that read, "Excuse our mess! We're renovating!" What the heck did they need to renovate? His last name was his last name. It wasn't like names changed, like history somehow alters itself.

I shook my head and walked away. *Crazies.*

The festival was crowded and just as alive as ever. *Don't these people have jobs they need to go to?*

The stage area was now turned into a viewing space for the Joan of Arc movie. Dogs and kids all ran around the park while their parents sat on blankets or fold-out campy chairs and watched the movie complete with popcorn, soda, and cotton candy.

I spotted Drake over by the food stands. He looked at me too, but I turned and walked the other way, not even waiting to see if he'd try to talk to me. Or what he'd do. I was right. He was wrong. End of story.

I moved toward the booths and spotted Courtney. A guy stood and talked to her. I recognized him as one of the freaks with the robe whose eyes turned white at the Wiccan meeting. He saw me coming before Courtney did and his face turned hard. *Wait. Shouldn't I be the pissed off one? Normal people don't usually roll their eyes in the back of their heads and practically laser beam weird symbols at others.*

I put on a polite smile anyway. "Hey guys."

"Hi," Courtney said, the chipper voice of hers mounting. "What are you up to?"

"I came to ask you a question actually. If you don't mind."

Courtney nodded at the boy and he walked away, nodding to Courtney and no motion at all to me, like I wasn't even a blip on his radar screen. It must be nice to have people do whatever you wanted them to with just a nod. If that worked, I would nod my mother a new freaking attitude. Or nod me a reason to not be scared of all this symbol shiz anymore.

"What can I help you with? Did you enjoy the meeting so much you're dying to come to another one?"

Her face screamed nice at me, making me want to vomit. I snickered. "Are you really that hard up for more witches?"

"A few of us are graduating this year and moving on to college. It's hard to have a group if there are only a few." Courtney shrugged.

I didn't join in her lament. This town could deal with a few less witches if you asked me. The only thing I wanted from her was the meaning behind the damn symbol. "Listen, Courtney, I was hoping you could help me out with something." The young witch lifted her eyebrows. "I'm not sure if I told you the other day. I've been kind of looking into my dad's death while I'm here."

"Your dad? Why?"

"Well, just because my mom's pretty much an epic failure at everything and I never knew any details. I'm just curious, you know?"

"David Perkins, right?"

My heart slammed once in my chest. "Yeah. So you've heard the story?"

"I don't think that's a good idea, Sarah." Courtney's short choppy hair ruffled in the wind. The undersides of her hair stood, the white of her scalp gleaming in the sunlight, making her dark hair seem black.

"Huh?"

She stood up straight, chin lifting. "I just mean, wouldn't you rather remember him as he was, not how he died?"

So sick of people acting like it was stupid to want to learn more about my dad, I squelched my original instinct to slap her. "I don't remember anything about him."

Like a seesaw, Courtney's whole body lifted from her tense, rigid frame. "Oh. Okay. So what do you want then?"

My throat constricted. I cleared it. I knew it would sound tight when it came out. I also knew I wasn't going to get anywhere by being nasty. "There's this symbol I keep seeing around. It's really weird, makes me feel funny…scared even."

"You already asked me about this symbol, didn't you?" She turned her back and rearranged the sale items at her family's booth.

"Yes. But I think you lied to me before…when I asked you about it."

She twisted back to me. "The sharp lines with the circle around it, right?" Courtney drew the shape in the air with her pointer finger.

"Yes."

"I didn't lie to you before. It's just that the relic is none of your business."

I stepped back, opening my mouth to speak. No words flowed.

"I'm not trying to be mean," Courtney insisted. "That symbol is sacred to the Wiccan religion. It's often used for us by people who do not understand us." She fanned through a deck of tarot cards arranged on the table and turned back to me.

Hmm, every time I ask her about the symbol, she gets twitchy. "Why do you get nervous when I ask you—?"

"I don't know, Sarah. Why do you?" Courtney shook her head and stepped away, maneuvering the crystals and Bohemian jewelry around the little table. "Are you a Jesus freak or something? Do you keep bringing up this symbol because you're trying to tell me that being a Wiccan is bad? That I'm going to hell? Because you have no idea what you're talking about."

I laughed. "Whoa. Calm down, Courtney. I have no idea what you're talking about. No, I am far from being a Jesus freak. The closest I ever get to church is when those 'Jesus freaks' stand on the corner by my coffee shop and yell at me that I'm a sinner and I'm going to hell once judgment day comes." Courtney stared until I stopped laughing. I couldn't help it. The image of me taunting somebody over religion was hysterical.

"So you really don't know what the symbol means?"

"No. I just keep seeing it everywhere."

Courtney slid her eyes from me, unsure whether she could trust me or not. "Just because we're Pagans, doesn't mean we worship the devil."

After a few seconds, I said, "Okay…you want to elaborate on that a little for me?"

"Historically, the symbol you keep mentioning was a symbol for the devil, but as Paganism evolved, now, it means changes. The changes we see in everything all around us."

"Changes?"

"Uh huh." Courtney nodded. "Changes."

The symbol meant changes. A stupid, inconsequential word. It wasn't the mark of the coven. It wasn't the mark of some witch that wanted to get me. It wasn't…anything. "So why does Marlene wear it around her neck and why was that symbol found on my dad's body…and why did I wake up this morning at Drake's house with that symbol painted on me if all it means is changes?"

After a confused look from Courtney, I told her the whole story. When I finished, she fanned the Tarot deck again. "What does Drake say?" Courtney asked.

I sighed. "Not much. He thinks I'm being stupid."

"I don't think you're being stupid, I just think it's hard for you to step back and examine things for what they really are. We're just a small town, Sarah. No one's trying to get one over on you. Or hurt you even. Maybe someone played a joke on you last night. Marlene's pretty ticked you're spending so much time with Drake."

Marlene did make sense. She wore the symbol around her neck. She could have drawn it on me when I somehow passed out in the woods. It would actually be kind of perfect. Hadn't she said Rose gave her the necklace as a symbol of her and Drake's relationship, of how they were meant to be together? "You think so?"

"Yeah."

"Well, I don't." I twirled toward the sound of the intruding voice. Jennie stood, hands on hips, eyes practically pulsing in her head. "It's not a joke, Sarah."

Courtney pulled out the Priestess voice. "Jennie, leave it alone."

She stood up straight, squaring her shoulders. "No."

"What's going on?" I asked.

"I think you need to hear what I have to say," Jennie said. "And I don't think you're crazy. I think you're exactly right."

I flicked back and forth between the two girls. They stared each other down. Neither flinched. "Fine," Courtney receded, turning a glare at me. "Just remember what I told you at the meeting." The high priestess' eyes burned into mine, as if she could send me a message telepathically.

I didn't need magic. I remembered when Courtney said Jennie was new and maybe a little crazy.

I nodded and walked away with the palm reader. "So, spill. What do you know about all this? And please, spare me the wrist grabbing this time."

"I am sorry about that. I was trying to get you away from them."

"From who?"

"Who do you think? The Witches of Eastwick over there. They are half a rung from being on top of crazy world."

"Wait. Aren't *you* a witch?" I dodged a bolting toddler, racing between us with a black balloon trailing behind on a red string.

"Yes, but I'm not like them."

"How so?"

"For starters, I don't dabble in the occult."

I snapped my head around to stare at Jennie. "The occult?"

"Yeah, freaky shit. Like *real* freaky shit."

"Like what?"

"Like it doesn't matter right now what they do!" Jennie's voice rose. "All that matters is that everybody's kept safe."

"What are you talking about?"

"Okay, I heard your entire conversation with Priestess Courtney." Her voice mocked the head witch's title, dousing it in acid. "That symbol does not mean change."

Jennie and I skirted behind a camping trailer before I pulled her to a stop. I needed answers. And now. "What does it mean?"

"It means exactly what Courtney said it means, but not historically. I have this Paganism book and looked it up myself, after I saw it used several times during the coven meetings. That symbol is the symbol for Satan. The devil. All the more reason for you to believe they're practicing dark magic."

"Dark magic?"

"Yes. Can't you keep up? The occult, Sarah. Dark magic. Nasty spells."

"Sorry, this—"

She waved her hands in front of me. "Shh. We don't have time. Where is the journal?" I stared at her and she frowned like she had to deal with a second grader who hadn't even learned to tie her shoes yet. "Your father's journal. Where is it?"

"Oh, um, Rose has it. It's in the library, I think. Why?"

"I think your dad knew something. That's why he was killed. And you're next."

****

"This is crazy, right? I mean really crazy." I stepped on the gas harder. The SUV roared underneath us until kicking into the next higher gear. "Why would you think they're into dark magic?"

"I moved here three months ago. For three months I have been watching this coven, participating in the meetings and doing research."

"Research?"

"Yeah." Jennie flattened herself against the back of the seat as I maneuvered around a wide curve. "Research. I'm pretty new to this whole Wicca stuff, but what they do is crazy. Everything I heard Courtney spout off to you about nature and blah, blah, blah is nothing like what happens in regular meetings."

"What do they do?"

She gave me a sideways glance and raised one eyebrow. "I've seen animal sacrifices."

I wrinkled my nose. "What?"

"As an offering to the gods. Mostly Hekate. And trust me, Hekate is one bad bitch."

"What do they want?"

"I don't know. I'm new, remember? I participate in everything, help channel my energy with theirs, but I don't really have an insider's voice. You know what I mean?"

"They keep you out of everything?" Jennie nodded, her hand tightened around the oh-shit-we're-gonna-flip grip. "Then, why do you stay?"

"I told you. Research. I thought I would have figured it out by now. I thought I could help them by seeing what they're doing and then telling somebody so they would make them stop."

"Who? Like the witch police?"

"I don't know. Maybe." Jennie said, throwing up her arms before she grabbed back on to the safe handle.

"But you haven't found anything that bad?"

"No. Like I said, I'm a newbie. A Wiccan Virgin. I don't really know what I'm supposed to be looking out for."

"Do you think it's possible that you're just freaking because maybe you don't understand what's going on at the meetings? That maybe this is all just some innocent miscommunication?"

"Maybe. I've tried to convince myself of that. Then I met you...and Drake."

"The palm reading?" I glanced at her sideways, trying to mask the doubt bubbling up inside me.

"I know I shouldn't have come at you like that." She shook her head. "It's the energy around Drake. It's...disturbing."

Out the window, I caught glimpses here and there of houses, barns, trees. Real, tangible things. Drake was real. He wasn't disturbing. He was...adorable? He wore his feelings all over his face. Energy or no energy, I would not believe he was anything but sincere. And a good kisser. And he made my stomach do flip flops. Okay, he was pretty much amazing.

What sucked was this magic crap. How could you believe in something you couldn't see?

"I know you don't want to believe, but take a look at this." Jennie dug through her bag and brought out a book, black and red imagery coated a five-pointed star. A pentagram. "Page thirty-two." The witch flipped through the pages and held it out to me.

I took it and propped the book up on the steering wheel, my gaze traveling back and forth between the road and the page. The lightning symbol took up the upper left half. I continued to scan. Some words were set in bold lettering and I picked them out right away. *Satan. Devil. Occult. Black Magic. Talisman.*

I threw the book back. "Why was this on me?" I pounded the steering wheel and looked to Jennie, who stared back blankly. We nodded together. This wasn't innocent. Far from innocent. We both felt it. A dead gut feeling.

When I switched my attention back to the road, I slammed on the brakes. The turn for Rose's place came up fast. "Damn. Is that how they drive where you're from?" Jennie asked. "I didn't think we were going to make it."

"Well, when somebody tells you you're going to die, you kind of get the need for urgency." A smirk crept across both our lips before jumping out of the SUV and jogging toward the huge Victorian. "I think I should mention. Rose doesn't want me in the library. And she's already caught me in there twice."

Jennie raised her eyebrows. "Lovely."

As soon as I entered the house, I took off for the library door and yanked at the handle. Relief flooded over me as it turned easily. I ran in and quickly described the journal to Jennie. "It's leather bound, with lettering on the front that says—"

"Um, problem here."

I turned. Jennie stood just before the entryway.

"What? Come on. My lease on life is running out here." I started to scan the bookcases.

"Sarah." Jennie's calm warning stilled the air like the eye of a tornado. I slowly turned, expecting Rose hovering somewhere nearby with a scowl and an eviction notice.

"What?"

"I can't come in."

"What do you mean you can't come in?"

"Watch." Jennie backed up a few steps and then stepped toward the open doorway, her palms outstretched. She stopped abruptly, facing me like she'd run into a wall.

"Funny. You can mime. Are you done making jokes now?"

"I'm not trying to be funny. It's a spell. Somebody put a spell on this room and made it so I can't get in."

"That's crazy. People can't do things like that, Jennie. It's not possible."

Jennie banged her fist on an invisible door, each time her fist didn't go any further, and each time, her skin smooshed out like she hit something solid and hard.

I lightly walked over, like carefully stepping on glass shards, one second away from being cut. "Do you think I can get out? Do you think I'm trapped in here?"

Jennie shrugged. "Only one way to find out."

I reached for the door like I would reach for an electric fence. I expected at any time to be stopped or stung or to keel over. When I got to the spot under where Jennie's palm rested, I stuck my finger out and it sliced right through. Jennie's fist still lay out, her skin white now with the pressure as she pushed against the invisible force. "Impossible."

I barged through, pushing Jennie out of the way and then we both stood on the outside looking in. "I do *not* want to get stuck in there."

"Too bad. I can't come in, which means you have to look for your dad's journal on your own. I think it might hold the answer."

"What if I get stuck in there and Rose comes home and finds me?"

"Who do you think put the spell on the room, Sarah?"

I shook my head. "No way. She's just an old lady. Besides, Courtney is the high priestess. She put the spell on the room."

"I know little Miss Courtney isn't working by herself. She always talks about someone she calls Mother."

"Maybe she's talking about her actual mother."

Jennie rolled her eyes. "Doubt it. That woman is a flake."

"Well, it's not Rose. Both Courtney and Drake say she isn't a witch."

"Oh, and where are those two right now?" I shrugged. "Exactly. I'm the one with you right now and I say she is. Well, she could be. And this is a powerful spell."

I was glad Jennie helped, but I felt like I had a little sister who always had to be right. Who knew exactly everything and loved reminding you of it. Inside, I scoffed at the thought of Rose casting spells and leaning over black cauldrons. The only thing she knew how to do was make Drake's favorite cookies. "So what do you want me to do?"

"Go inside and search for the journal." She pointed to the first bookcase. "If you can't find it we'll…figure something else out."

I stepped tentatively up to the doorway. *This is crazy.* I broke free again. Whatever the spell was let me in, but not Jennie. Weird. I picked up the pace and went straight for the first wood shelf and rummaged through it, looking for Dad's name on the covers. "It's so hard. All these journals are exactly alike."

"Get me one." I tossed her the journal I just pulled from the shelf. Jennie's fingers silently crashed against the wall and she yanked them back in pain, without the book.

"Sor-ry," I called out, still immersed in the hundreds of leather-bound journals.

Jennie tried to shake the pain from her hand and then bent over. She was able to grab a corner of the book and pull it across the shield.

A whistle sounded from within the house. A happy go-lucky tune. I froze, then ran for the door. I sighed a sweet, deep sigh of relief when the spell didn't keep me from exiting. Jennie closed the library door quietly and tugged me away. With one hand, she hid the journal in the waistband of her shorts and pulled her t-shirt out over it as we left the house.

"Quit grabbing me like that," I warned, snatching my wrist away.

"Sorry. I didn't want your aunt to see me in there. She would figure out we were up to something." Jennie walked straight for the passenger-side door. "Where are we going?"

"Up the road a little ways. We need to get out of here and then we can pull over and talk."

I jogged around the backside of the Escalade. My phone buzzed in my pocket. I flipped it open and found a text from Drake waiting for me:

Where are you? Courtney says you're with Jennie. Be careful. She's not who you think.

But she's the only one willing to help. I exited out of it.

"Who was that?" Jennie asked as I opened the car door.

"My mother. She hates it that I'm here."

"I bet." Jennie's dribble of fingers across the dashboard marked her impatience. I turned the key and took a right, knowing exactly where we needed to go now. Drake was at the festival, obviously talking with Courtney, which meant his grandfather was at home. Alone.

I needed to talk to him alone.

Chapter Twenty

1639

Thomas moved Isabella behind him, his chest heaving. "Father, Isabella Lynne and I are leaving." She peeked around her lover's shoulder. Magistrate Ludington smiled. "We are leaving tonight. We will be together."

"My son." He motioned for Thomas to come closer. The young man stood his ground, chin up and chest out. The elder man smirked. "I believe I have some information that may change your mind."

"There is nothing you can say—"

"This girl is a witch!" His face transitioned from smirk to sneer in an instant, the anger pulsing out of him. "Why else do you think you fell in love with her? She has been using her magical abilities on you. She tricked you into loving her."

Isabella and Thomas both gasped and Thomas moved ever so slightly away from her. She heard her mother sobbing from inside their tiny cottage. Hands from behind clasped down on Isabella, breaking her free of Thomas' loosened grasp, and then dragged her to face the man she loved along with his father. "What are the evidences against her?"

"This!" Mr. Ludington dug in his pockets and threw items down on the grass before them all. Isabella did not recognize the contents. They looked like leaves and herbs.

She fought back against her imprisoner. His iron grip dug into the flesh at her wrists he held behind her back. "What is this? I do not know what this is," she sobbed.

"They are ingredients you use for spells. Root from a honeysuckle tree and thyme," Mr. Ludington explained.

"Isabella could not be what you say. She is a God-fearing young woman."

"You say this because she tricks you. I found these items in the forest when she placed a spell on you to meet her outside of town."

"Father, she did not put a spell on me." Thomas looked from Isabella to the magistrate. "I just happened upon her there."

"And still that does not seem odd to you? She was in the woods, at night, when the moon was full in the sky and waiting for you?" The judge looked up into the night and yelled, "Is this not suspicious behavior?"

The door to the house banged open and Mr. Lynne appeared, afraid, but with teeth gritted like a stalking lion. "Give me my daughter." The farmer's fist tore into the face of Mr. Austen allowing Isabella to run to her father's side. The magistrate and Thomas came together in front of them. Mr. Lynne pleaded, "She is not what you say. You only fear for your reputation. Why cannot these two love if they wish to? Why cannot these two be together if they want to?"

Mr. Ludington laughed aloud. "I do not care that your family is poor, Lynne. I care that she has bewitched my son. This witch has tricked him into loving her."

"That is nonsensical!" More men from the hunting party gathered around. Fires from their torches sent flames leaping upwards mixed with black smoke. Mrs. Lynne's cries mounted in her daughter's bedroom. Isabella clutched her father's arm and he patted it in reassurance. "Drop this now. We are all learned men here. We need not quarrel or make up stories."

"The only one speaking nonsense is you. Everybody here, in this circle, this one has you tricked." The judge inclined his head toward Isabella. "I can see it in your eyes. You are dazed, willing to believe everything she says. Her powers are great. They are worse than any witch I and yourselves have come across. I am sure she must be the direct descendant of Satan. His hold is on her and she will snare us all in it."

Mr. Lynne ran at the magistrate. Thomas stepped in front, hands up. Isabella screamed, "Thomas." The young man wavered, looking between his love and her father. "You know me. I am just Isabella…just your Isabella."

"Close your ears!" Mr. Ludington bellowed. All around, men dropped their torches and placed their palms hard over their ears. Everyone but her father and Mr. Ludington. Everyone, even Thomas. "She casts a spell before us now. Quick, Austen, tie the cloth around her mouth." Mr. Austen fumbled, not wanting to hear the incantations of an accused witch. He finally removed a white cloth from his pocket and came at Isabella. Thomas watched, his hands covering his ears. He would not hear anything Isabella said, even if she did speak. The tears running down her face said it all.

She stood tall when the man came at her with the bind, but her father threw himself in the middle again until the magistrate tackled him from behind, placing his heavy body over his. "Do not struggle Lynne, or you will be punished." Isabella swooned, her insides heavy within her. "Look!" Mr. Ludington exclaimed. "She loses her powers because we listen not to her spells."

Isabella's lids drooped as her body buckled under her. Thomas was the last face she saw. His hands finally came away from his ears, anger flecking his eyes as her mouth was stuffed with cloth.

****

Isabella woke to complete blackness. If she had not felt her eyes open, she would not be able to tell whether she stared at something or at the back of her lids. The earthen floor was dank, her cheek rested against the dampness of it. Her mouth stuck together and when she opened her jaw to wet her lips and insides, her tongue met with the grit of dirt. Her arm throbbed, pain shot through it as she moved to sit, teeth clenching over the hard grains in her mouth. She spit out and felt a wetness hit her leg.

Reaching up, she brushed dirt from her cheek. It stung to the touch and swelled underneath her. She wiped at it, eager to remove the dirt from her, pulling her fingertips away in shock a few times as pain shot through her.

Isabella looked up, searching for any sign of light. She found nothing. No cracks where the moon or the sun might shine through. No flicker of yellow from a candle. Despite the complete darkness, she knew where she was.

Magistrate Ludington's gaol.

The cellar of his house hid the miscreants of society before they were tried and punished. Where they housed the witches his parties caught, where they kept them before they burned away their sins.

Burned.

With that thought, she fainted.

****

A groan spurred Isabella awake again. She had no sense of time or hour. Only her begging stomach consumed her waking life.

A sliver of light illuminated part of the cell. Nothing but brown dirt and gray stone met her. The light decreased again as a door to her left shut. A jumping flame cast wood stairs in shadows and light as feet descended them.

Isabella blinked her eyes, the light stinging them. The figure before her was a blur, like a distorted reflection from the stream on her family's farm.

She could not see who came to her, though she smelled food. Her stomach ate at her, like a leach sucking up blood. "P-p-please…" Isabella reached out to the shadowy figure. A bowl was placed by her lying head, under her nose.

Isabella tried to move, but her limbs failed her. Tears slipped from her eyes. The figure swore, bent down, and picked up the spoon. She opened her mouth and hot liquid fell into it, some running into her mouth and some dripping from her lips to the dirt floor. "Th-thank you."

"You need to sit and feed yourself." The voice stoic, brave. It sent a spark through her.

"I do not know—"

A hand gripped her arm and pulled her up. Her head hit the rock wall behind her and a whimper escaped. "There."

Isabella breathed in deep, her head swirled around her, and then faded to black.

****

Isabella's eyes fluttered open. The smell of food consumed her unconscious mind. The growling of her stomach could not be ignored. Her eyes finally landed open for good. A candle and a bowl of stew lay in front of her. She moved her aching muscles and reached out for the bowl. They complained, but she pushed through.

Her fingers shook as she brought the spoon to her mouth. The stew, though cold, soothed her. Her stomach rumbled as it finally slipped down her throat. She spooned mouthful after mouthful into her until she scraped bottom and then emptied the liquid into her mouth, tipping the bowl to her lips.

"Here." Isabella jumped. The shadows spoke to her. She strained her eyes and saw nothing. A piece of bread landed by the candle. Isabella tore off a piece and stuffed it in her mouth, chewing it down. "I suppose you are hungry. It has been three days."

The food, the company, the recognition of his voice spurred her heart. "Have you come to save me?"

She thought she heard a catch in his voice, or maybe it was a sound of protest. "No."

Isabella stuffed another piece of bread in her mouth, holding back a sob that crept up. "Why are you sitting where I cannot see you?"

"My father says I am to stay away from you."

"And why do you not listen?"

Grinding of pebbles on dirt sounded as Thomas came at her. He crawled on all fours, his face coming to rest inches from hers. She scrambled back and hit her head on the rock again. "Because I have to know how it happened. How did you take over my Isabella?" His breath caught, barely choking out the last words.

"I am your Isabella. I do not know of what you are speaking. I am just me. Just Isabella."

Thomas raised his hand up and brought it down across her cheek. She dropped the last piece of bread from her hand and a foreign liquid dripped in her mouth. She spit out bread and blood at his feet. He jumped back and then looked at her again. "Do not lie to me."

"I am not a witch!" She turned to him, her eyes cold, face leaking in rage. "I am just me."

Thomas brought his hand up again. Isabella cowered, dropping her face between her legs and brought up her hands as a shield. His hand thudded to the earthen ground.

"Pray believe me, Thomas. I have no magical abilities." Her words choked back by tears and breaks in her chest.

"They found things in your desk."

"I told you about the writing I found before. Did I not? 'Tis Mrs. Shipton. She has turned you away from me. Turned everybody against me."

"My father trusts her. She says herself that she saw you in the woods."

"Because she called me there. But that was a dream, Thomas." She spoke the words, they flew from her mouth.

"When did they take you from me?" His face peered up, his eyes searching the ceiling or perhaps above it, way above it.

She said the only thing that came to her. "When you followed them and not your heart."

ERIN BUTLER

Chapter Twenty-One

Present Day

"Stay here." I steered the car into Drake's driveway. Jennie mumbled under her breath, but she stayed. I didn't want two people to interrogate the old man. Jennie was forceful, a brute even. Drake would never talk to me again. Hell, I'd have a heck of a time convincing him to do so now as it was.

I knocked on the door. After some shuffling and an unmistakable sound of footsteps accompanied by a cane, the door opened. An old man peered around the huge wood door. The first thing I noticed were his eyebrows. Long silver and black strands curled up over his wrinkly forehead, marking him an old man. My heart sank. Could I really pepper this guy for information? He was fragile, cute, with cracks in his old skin—a grandfather.

"Hello?" His voice came out phlegm-filled.

And my voice came out soft, and sweet. Not the way I envisioned interrogating the man who may hold clues to how my dad died. "Hello. Mr. Connors? I'm Sarah. Drake's friend?"

"Oh yes. Sarah." The old man nodded and opened the door wider. "Drake's told me all about you. Come in dear."

I stepped through the big wooden entryway. "Thank you."

The house was filled with antiques—ceramic knickknacks, metal plates, country paintings, doilies—the epitome of an old person's house and it was all accentuated with dark wood. Dark wood door frames. Dark wood floors. Dark wood cabinets and molding. So dark inside, it could have been nighttime. The old man snickered. "I heard you had a rough night the other night. I hope you're feeling better."

"I am," I lied, wondering if Drake invented a story about me sleeping over or used the truth.

"Drake's not here. I do expect him any moment though." Mr. Connors turned and walked off toward the living room straight ahead.

My heart pulsed in my chest. "Oh. Well, I can come back if you want." I half-hoped he'd say yes.

"No, no, that's okay. I figured you would be coming by to talk to me sooner or later."

I didn't reply and the air settled in heavy now. I shut the door and the darkness swallowed me in it as I made my way through the house.

The wobbly old man used his cane to steady himself as he lowered into an armchair. "I was just wondering when." He sighed as his backside finally landed on the cushion of the chair and then he propped his glasses further up on his nose. "Have a seat." I sat on a blue and white plaid sofa. Drake's grandfather started right up. The sides of his eyes etched in years of wisdom, in smiles and frowns. "It is hard when we lose loved ones. I lost my wife you know, many years ago. Drake was a toddler." He motioned toward the mantle. Pictures lined up across the jutting stone and a huge ivory canvas crowned everything. "And my son and daughter-in-law. Drake's parents. I am sure he told you."

I nodded. "I am sorry for your losses." The extra s choked me up.

"As I am sorry for yours. And whatever part I may have played in it."

"That's exactly what I want to ask you about."

"Well, ask away."

I figured a straightforward question was the best way to go about it. Like a Band-Aid. One quick swipe and I would have my answer. "Did you kill my father?"

He didn't seem surprised or taken back. He tapped his cane a couple times and said, "You know, I've been asking Drake to bring you over here since he told me who you were and who you were related to. This was back even before he knew about…this."

"He says you're too sick to see anybody."

Mr. Connors' yellow-tinged eyes stared at the wall behind me. "Too sick? I guess you can call it that." He chuckled a little, the amusing tinge stuck in his phlegm-filled throat. A half-laugh, half-cough filled the small sitting room. "I don't know how much detail I can give you."

"Did the cops ask you not to say anything?"

The old man waved his vein-rippled hand, tossing the words aside. "No. It's an old man's memory my dear." He made the hacking sound again. "I fear memory has left me with only the absolute worst moments of my life." He brought out a folded blue handkerchief from his pocket and wiped his mouth. "I can tell you for sure that I was not the one that killed your father."

"He was dead already then?"

"Yes."

The corners of my eyes moistened. Than it is like I thought. Something much worse happened. I had hoped, maybe, that I was tormenting myself, jumping to awful conclusions. Now I know for sure. "Thank you." I wiped the tears away with my fingers. "This might sound strange, Mr. Connors, but do you know if anyone else may have killed my father?"

"I'm afraid I can't answer that."

"Of course," I said. Stupid. What was he? Psychic?

"No, I mean, I *can't* answer that."

I nodded, my mind a mixture and jumble of sporadic thoughts, and lifted my eyes away from Mr. Connors. His eyes were too sad to look at too long.

I took stock of the room around me again, studying the fireplace photos more closely. There was one with Drake in a graduation cap and gown, standing in between two very happy people. A man and a woman. Drake's parents, I guessed, glowed with pride. The picture stuck out to me as a beacon, and I wondered if Cici would make time to come to my own graduation next year.

Up above that, on the canvas, was a family tree. A huge, bold tree painted on it, with a thick brown trunk and gnarly sprouting branches holding generation after generation's names. There weren't that many branches actually for going back so many years. It must have been only immediate family. No cousins or aunts and uncles cluttered it up. There were places ready and waiting for the next generation. Drake's name was there, waiting for his wife and child.

I mentally imagined my own. Mine branched even less than his. I could only put four people on there that I knew of. My mom, my dad, myself, and Dad's aunt on a little off shoot branch that curled up and around. Only four people. "Sir, I need to ask you one more question. Do you know anything about a weird Wiccan symbol? I keep seeing it everywhere."

Mr. Connors' fingertips curled on the arm of the chair, the fabric gathering beneath him. "An S?"

"No. A lightning bolt with a circle around it."

"I can't say—" The front door creaked as it swung open on its hinges. Mr. Connors stopped mid-sentence. Footsteps plotted a course for the living room.

"Drake, did you have a good time at the fair?" Drake moved into view, his back facing me as he walked up to his grandfather and kissed his forehead.

"Hey Pops, yeah everything was good." He squeezed the older man's hand.

Mr. Connors motioned to me. "Don't be rude. Say hello to your friend."

Drake turned. His face fell. "What are you doing here?"

"I—"

"Now you calm down boy, you hear? This nice young lady came over here looking for you. Which you should be grateful for by the way. She's a catch. And she's had to sit here and listen to the ramblings of an old man while you sat around causing a raucous with your friends."

Drake turned and smiled at his grandfather. "A raucous, Pops?"

The old man hacked and laughed again. Drake stood over him, hovering while Mr. Connors tried to wave him away. The episode didn't last very long and I found myself laughing at the sight of the two of them.

"What?" Drake asked.

"She's laughing at you. You act like I'm some fine porcelain china. Didn't I tell you? You aren't getting spit when I die. There's nothing to give." He winked at me. "So why do you keep trying to ensure your trust fund?"

Drake walked away and plopped down next to me, my shoulders still heaved with silent giggles. "So you finally met her, huh Grandpa?"

"Yes, and she's a heck of a lot prettier than you made her out to be."

Drake chose to ignore him and stared at me with wide eyes. "Did you guys talk?"

I reached out and put my hand on Drake's leg and nodded. Drake's grandfather said, "I guess that's what two human beings do with each other when their mouths open and sounds come out."

"I love you, Pops."

"I love you too, Drake. Now don't sit around here wasting time talking to an old man, take her out." He winked at me and grabbed a remote from the table beside him and turned on the television sitting in the back corner of the room. When Drake didn't move, he wiggled his fingers at him, spurring us into motion.

Drake shook his head and laughed, then helped me to my feet. "He's great," I said as Drake led me to the door.

Passing once again through the house, seeing all the relics and family heirlooms, I realized something. Things *are just things unless they're attached to people.* This whole house was filled with history. What ultimately mattered though, was people like Drake's grandfather. They had history all bound up in them. They practically lived it. They knew the stories, we didn't.

If I had to be completely honest with myself, I'd realize Drake and his grandfather went through a hell of a lot more than me. Drake lost both his parents and his grandmother already. Yeah, so I lost my dad. Big deal. I didn't even know him. Right now, he was just some spot on my family tree. That didn't mean I couldn't mourn him and shouldn't mourn him. It didn't even mean I couldn't feel bad about not knowing him, but what really mattered?

Drake opened the door and I peered outside. Jennie was gone. She probably freaked when Drake pulled up and decided to hoof it.

"Yeah. I told you he was pretty great."

"I never meant to say he wasn't. I just had to know."

"I get that. Well, I get that now." He pointed back inside the house. "He made me see it."

"He's a smart man."

He stopped me as we stepped off the porch steps. "So where's Jennie?"

I pointed to the SUV. "She was there."

Drake looked over. "She wasn't when I pulled in."

"I don't know. I left her there when I went in the house. I figured you would never forgive me if both of us went in to talk to your grandfather."

He kicked at the pebble-strewn driveway. "I'm sorry we fought."

"Yeah, me too." I took a step toward him.

"I don't think you should be seeing Jennie," he said as I slid my arms around him, resting them on his shoulder blades.

"Why?"

"Because Courtney said she's not a good witch." I stared back at him, eyes a blinking cursor on a computer screen. "I mean literally, she's not a *good* witch. She does black magic."

"Funny. That's what Jennie says about Courtney and her little coven."

"I grew up with Courtney and those guys. They don't do that kind of stuff." He looped his hands around my hips.

"Animal sacrifices?"

"Animal sacrifices? Ha. That's a good one. I think Jennie's watched too many scary movies."

"I don't know, Drake. These things aren't adding up."

"You're still worried about the symbol?"

"Yes. Jennie thinks my life is in danger. Your grandpa said he didn't kill my dad, he was already dead. I don't believe that heart attack crap. He was young."

Drake nodded. "I admit, it is kinda weird. But just weird, not life threateningly weird."

"Will you help me figure out what's going on?"

"Help you figure out who the crazy person is? In the town that I love? Yeah. Sure. Sounds like fun."

"I see where you get your humor now." *People and what they stand for are what matter.* "And thank you. For helping me."

****

We couldn't agree on a suspect list as we sat in a far corner booth in the "worst diner in town" as Drake put it, which "is perfect because nobody will be there".

I wrote down names and Drake went through and crossed them off, relying on his true detective skills. "Please, I was in Kindergarten with her" and "Boy Scouts with this one." The one he crossed out until you couldn't see the loops of my writing underneath it, was Rose.

"No way."

"Jennie thinks she's a witch."

Drake scribbled down Jennie's name at the top of the list. "For starters, her name goes here. No way is Rose a witch. You have no idea who she even is. You just met her. You have no idea who all of these people are," he said, scanning his finger down the list.

"Maybe that's why I can see them more objectively." I folded up the paper and put it in my pocket.

Drake took a bite of his burger and then let the processed meat drop back on his plate. His face mashed together as he chewed. "Abigail's is so much better."

"Spies can't afford to be seen. …Oh my god, I've got it. We'll spy on a Wiccan meeting. That's how we'll find out whose bad and whose not."

He smirked. "Who wants to kill you and who doesn't?"

"Exactly."

ERIN BUTLER

Chapter Twenty-Two

1639

"Don't do this to me John!" A cry from the closed door carried through the wood and down into the dark interior. The door banged open and a bundle bounced off the stairs and rolled down, ending in a contorted heap at the bottom.

The judge stuck his head in and stared straight at his son. "Get away from her."

Thomas shuffled back. "Who is that?" He pointed at the tangle of clothing.

"Mrs. Shipton."

"But you—"

"Get up here now boy! Away from that witch!"

Isabella reached out for Thomas. He slapped her hand away. "Do not touch me."

"Do not leave me in here with her. You know what she is. Please!"

Thomas stood and strode over to the steps. His father patted his back as the shaft of light emptied, leaving two women, two convicted witches in the dank cell.

Mrs. Shipton stirred. She groaned and lifted herself up to a sitting position, rubbing her head and shoulders. The waning candle caught her eye and she stared at Isabella. "I warned you. You did not listen."

Isabella ignored her. Bringing her feet up in front of her, she laid her head down upon them and wrapped herself up.

"I told you he would hurt you. I told your mother so that she might stop you. I knew that he would do this to you. I knew his displeasure with your family."

"Who?" Isabella winced as her voice carried to the other woman. She did not mean to speak.

"Who?" She scoffed. "John Ludington. I knew he was not fond of you, no matter what good things people said of you. He has issues with money. Your parents' lack of money."

"My father works hard."

"And has nothing to show for it." Isabella saw a slight raise of the woman's shoulders from across the room, her features contorting in pain. "That makes him still the same poor farmer."

Isabella made no answer, resting her head down on the tops of her knees again. Cries started to echo throughout the cell. Isabella tried to shut it out, to smother her ear against her knee to drown the sound. "I know I should not have done what he told me to." Mrs. Shipton's weak gasps raked in air. "But I love John. And he loves me too."

Chapter Twenty-Three

Present Day

"Shh…Jeez, haven't you ever had to sneak around before."

"No."

"Oh, that's right. I forgot. I'm with Mr. Squeaky Clean over here." I treaded softly over the branches and leaves as we walked through the woods to spy on tonight's Wiccan meeting.

"I'm sure you have so much experience doing this."

I lifted my shoulders. "Not exactly this." I knew the way around my house in the dark though, that was for sure.

I ducked down as we approached the clearing. We had been walking to the right of the dirt road. As we got closer though, we moved further in so no one would see us. I motioned for Drake to get lower. He complied, but his entire face smirked. He thought this was dumb. Maybe it was. I really didn't care.

Drake and I settled down in some leaves, our backs against enormous trees whose leaves reached for the sky. We could just see the clearing through a tangle of branches ahead of us. That was fine with me; I was more interested in hearing their voices, not watching cruel animal sacrifices or anything else the disturbed Crazies wanted to do.

Drake twisted toward me, the leaves cracking underneath his weight. "Sarah?"

I stared through the clearing; a few coven members had arrived and talked amongst each other. "Hmm?"

"Sarah?"

I couldn't quite make out what they were saying. They kept their voices low. I did hear mention of the word Mother, as Jennie said. I was about to suggest we move a little closer when Drake's lips landed on mine as I turned. I froze. He urged my mouth open with his and I kissed him back.

Soon, the voices, the coven, were far away. We embraced each other and our once light kisses turned deep and needy. We broke apart, breathing heavy. "Where did that come from?" I asked. "You said you weren't going to kiss me again."

"You weren't paying any attention to me, and I needed to know if you liked me."

"You couldn't just ask?"

"I needed to know the truth."

"And you think I'm a liar?"

Drake paused, and, taking my face in his hands, he brought me closer to him. Our lips touched again. A soft, sweet kiss that turned my insides to butterflies. He pulled away and searched my eyes again. "I knew if you liked me, you'd kiss me. If you didn't…" He shrugged.

"What?" I asked, moving my hips closer to his, eager to kiss him again.

His voice caught in his throat. "I don't know…you'd probably punch me or something." I bent my head and kissed Drake's cheek, then the side of his mouth. His lips moved underneath mine. This was what life was about. "I really like you, Sarah."

"I really like you too."

"God guys, get a room." I jumped and spotted Jennie peering at us through some branches she forced out of her way. Her face crinkled together like a rotten apple. "Aren't you here to do some spying? The meeting's that way." She shot a glance through the woods. "It's already starting. I'm going to do some work from the inside. By the way, I had to apologize to Priestess Courtney so I could come to tonight's meeting." She shot me a look. A look which made it clear she was not happy at all about having to say she was sorry. Then, she took off, shaking her head and walked around to the road before striding up next to the hooded group.

I looked back at Drake, our legs still twisted together. I got a flash of his abs before he tugged his shirt down and rearranged his shorts. "How does she know we're here?" His face was red and stone-like.

"I texted her."

"I don't like her."

Now that our lips weren't on each other's, I felt hot and my insides buzzed. I looked down at the ground, an annoying thought repeatedly poked my brain, reminding me I had more important things to do right now than kiss Drake. Though it was a nice distraction.

He pulled on my sneaker. "Come here." I twisted and sat in between his legs, laying my back against his chest. He folded his arms around me. "Just because we're acting like Nancy Drew doesn't mean we can't...have fun."

He kissed my neck and no matter how much I wanted him to keep going, I turned to him and kissed his lips. "We should really pay attention to this."

He pecked me on the mouth. "You act like someone's going to hurt you or something."

I laughed and snuggled back into his arms, eyes straight ahead toward the clearing.

Courtney was at the meeting now.

She drew the circle and everybody stepped in, hands linked. Each coven member dressed in the same long robes that descended to their knees. Courtney placed white candles around the circle and lit them. When she moved next to her fellow witches, they bent down in front of her, their foreheads touching the blades of grass.

Back at the altar, Courtney bent over in the same fashion, murmuring words I couldn't quite understand. She rocked back and forth, eyes staring down to the ground. I craned my neck to see past a leafy branch.

None of the witches moved. I couldn't tell which one was Jennie. The stupid robes made each witch undeterminable from one another. I wished we'd made some sort of secret sign language so I'd comprehend what was happening. Looking back at Drake, he shrugged his shoulders and tightened his grip around me, burying his nose in my hair. He was some help.

Courtney rocked some more. Her voice rising and lowering in tune. Wind blew the flames on the candles low before they shot right back up again. The flames grew higher, fueled by the wind, looking like mini torches. The high priestess stopped and rose to her feet. The other witches fidgeted as Courtney smiled down. "Rise," she said, voice powerful.

The coven members rose, their knees still planted firmly on the ground, and tilted their heads to see what Courtney revealed. She brought up an object to her face, and a solid wall of some sort interrupted my view. I unwound Drake's hands from around me and rose to my knees, mimicking the actions of the witches. Courtney laughed—an astonished, amused laugh. "It's Mother!"

The coven looked around at one another, all smiles except one. I picked Jennie out now. Instead of looking up at her high priestess, Jennie stared into the woods and locked eyes with me. Her shoulders lifted as if to say 'I have no freaking clue'.

"Whose mother?" Drake asked.

"No idea. We need to find out."

Drake stood. I pulled him down again, bringing my finger to my lips. We both peered back through the darkening forest. Courtney held the object high, waving it around toward the sky. "It's her. It's really her." She brought the square back to her face and smiled. "I'm glad you have come."

I turned toward Drake and lifted my eyebrows. He shook his head. Courtney turned the object around. It was glass. A mirror, actually. The green of the leaves in front of us showed on the shiny exterior. The high priestess threw back her hood and walked up to each witch, facing the reflective surface toward every one of them.

The coven pulsed with excitement and agitation. When Courtney got to the witches nearest the edge of the woods where Drake and I hid, I could recognize some of them from the other night in the reflective surface. Their eyeballs stayed intact this time, their faces flashing with happiness.

"What the hell is going on?" I whispered.

"No idea."

"They're only looking at themselves."

"I see this."

When Courtney got to Jennie, the young witch mimicked that of her coven. Her eyes lit up and she nodded. *Did she actually see something?*

"This is crazy," Drake laughed out. His voice rose.

"Shh."

"No. Come on, Sarah. They know we're watching. That's why they're acting like this. They're playing a joke on me. Well, har har...too—"

I clasped my fingers over Drake's mouth and brought a finger to my lips again, threatening him with my eyes. I turned back toward the circle to find Courtney at the altar, bent over, pouring something on a white candle and dropping little leaves on it. She then lit it. The flame rose, higher than any other around the circle, yet the wind calmed to a tortoise speed.

"Mother needs me to bring her." Courtney grabbed a piece of paper from her pile of things and wrote with a pen. She folded the paper up, taking care to crease the lines just so and then placed it under the candle. She turned to face in Jennie's direction and started to chant.

> *If you are turning toward me*
> *know I turn also to you,*
> *If you are thinking of me*
> *know I think also of you,*
> *If you are saying my name*
> *know that I say your name,*
> *and call you to me*
> *Marlene*
> *Marlene*

The other witches joined in for one last *Marlene*. A piece of my hair flew into my face. I moved the strands around my ear, still staring at the witch circle. Each concentrated ahead, their faces a marble of emotion. Even Jennie stood transfixed. She did not try to catch my eye again.

Drake twitched beside me while I sat completely still, heart palpitating as cold blood rushed throughout me. The wind tore leaves from trees and sprinkled them about. Some landed on the dark robes. One even landed on one of the white candles and disintegrated into smoke. Poof, it was gone. It was free for only a few seconds, then left nothing but air as it was carried away with the wind.

The longer the coven sat motionless, the more nerves raked through me. I didn't even bother to look at Drake. His hand twitched a few times, but I was sure he sat as hypnotized as I was. *No way will he be able to tell me there's nothing going on now.*

The vibration of a car hummed its way through the forest. I heard the ting of the suspension as it bounced along the mud ruts of the old work road. I swiveled my head. A white car pulled up behind the other vehicles.

Drake careened his head. "Ho-ly shit."

"What?" I whispered.

He squinted. A figure stepped out of the car and walked blithely up the rock spackled road. It was a she, I could tell. She jingled her keys in her hand before placing them in her pockets.

"Oh. My. God."

"What?" I grabbed Drake's wrist.

Drake dragged his eyes across every inch of the trail the girl walked. "Marlene," he whispered. As she entered the circle, a collective release of breath shocked the coven into moving again.

"No." I shook my head. "No way."

Drake nodded. "Trust me."

ERIN BUTLER

Chapter Twenty-Four

1639

The sobs echoing around the darkened room once the candle sputtered out were endless. Isabella fell into disturbed sleep and woke to whispered cries or choked wails. She made no move for the woman, the witch, though her heart melted away beneath her smock.

Might she have done the same for Thomas?

A creak of the wood reverberated through the small cellar. A shaft of soft light drifted down on the earthen floor. Mrs. Shipton's cries hushed to whimpers. Feet descended the groaning steps until the whole figure revealed itself at the bottom.

Magistrate Ludington.

He turned to Isabella. "You."

Mrs. Shipton cried out again. "You know she is not...you know she—"

"Silence!" He twisted to face the witch and bent over. His hand smacked her cheek and trailed across every inch of her lips and nose. "Witch! Do not speak your blasphemy!"

Isabella tightened herself into a little ball in front of the wall, wishing she could hide herself in it. He turned to her. "We are ready for you."

"John, no, you cannot do this." Mrs. Shipton crawled across the floor, blood flowing from her nose, and grabbed at his breeches. Mr. Ludington raised his hand again and though she cowered, she still held tight to the fabric. "You are a good man. You cannot do this."

The judge paused before kneeling in front of Mrs. Shipton, tears running freely down her face, begging him to stop. He reached out and the old woman flinched. He cupped the side of her head in his hands. "What would you have me do, Love?"

Mrs. Shipton squeezed her eyes, more tears sprung forth. "Save us. Save us now."

"But that will only help you." He leaned forward and kissed her, his lips moving softly on hers. Isabella's heart clenched, reminding her of the only kiss she shared with Thomas. "What of me? Be branded a liar, a joke? No. That will not happen. You will burn before then."

Chapter Twenty-Five

Present Day

Marlene chatted with Courtney like it was the most normal thing in the world for her to be the center of attention at a witch ritual. She tossed her hair and still smacked gum. "Sorry, I'm late. I totally forgot I was going to come today and then…" Her voice trailed, making an imaginary non-excuse for her random appearance.

It wasn't necessary. Courtney summoned her here. Courtney and the others summoned her. I saw it with my own eyes. I was glad I did because if I hadn't, I wouldn't have believed it. I heard the name Marlene, watched as the white car pulled up and Marlene stepped out. I heard the words. The coven's magic summoned a person.

Impossible. Unfortunately, it wasn't.

As Marlene talked, Courtney grabbed an object and fiddled with it. A tethered, blowing leaf invaded my vision so I bowed my head. At Marlene's retreating words, Courtney held it up. A toy doll made with plain, ivory colored canvas, which bore rope tied all around the body.

Marlene stood dumbly, staring at Courtney with unseeing eyes. "It is done, Mother." Courtney brought the mirror and the doll together and dropped them. The mirror hit first, shattering. The clatter of the glass ripped through the silent forest and then the doll thudded on top. Courtney grabbed the doll from the wreckage and stored it away under her robe.

Zombified Marlene stood while Courtney went around and undid the circle, calling goodbye to the goddesses and blowing out candles. Afterward, she stuck her hand through the crook of Marlene's elbow and led her away. Once they broke the plane of the invisible sphere, Marlene asked, "Oh, did I miss it?" A puppy frown broke her marble stature.

"Yeah, I'm sorry girl. We couldn't wait."

"Oh alright. They hugged by the road and Marlene skipped off, waving to everybody before she got in her car and drove away. The other witches did the same. All of them, even Jennie, retreated to their cars and drove off like this was any other normal night.

When the clunk of the last car shuddered over the knotty, hardened mud, I finally turned to look at Drake. "We've got a mess on our hands," he said. He interlaced his fingers with mine.

"You're right about that one." As we walked out of the leafy jungle, I jumped at every crowing bird and whispering insect. Drake steered me toward the old work road, helping me keep my balance while we trekked over the hardened ruts. "You saw that right?" I asked. "All of it? I mean, they called Marlene and then she drove up, like, what? Less than five minutes later?"

"Uh huh."

"Is this usual Adams behavior…or is this town getting crazier by the day?"

Drake blew a hard breath out his nose. "This is…this is…nothing I've seen before."

"But it had to of, right? Don't you see this all adding up somehow? Your local crazy coven o' witches actually has powers. The detective said my dad was found with a Wiccan symbol on him when he died. I mean, come on. What more evidence do we need?"

"A lot." Drake tightened his grip around my fingers. "I know it adds up all nice and neat in your head, but I can't wrap my brain around this. I grew up with those guys. It's not like I've seen people walk around casting spells here."

"Maybe you weren't looking hard enough."

Drake tossed his head from side to side. "This is crazy. What we're thinking is crazy."

"Maybe. But, I think we both can agree now." I stopped in mid-stride and held back on Drake's arm. He spun to face me. "I'm in deep trouble." I paused, mouth dropping wide, as recognition sliced through me. "Do you think that's what they did to me?"

"What?"

"I blacked out. I woke up. The symbol painted on my forehead. Oh my god, Drake. They put a spell on me. They lured me here, did who knows what to me, and then sent me on my way again." My hands trembled as I reached out for him. He took me in his arms. "And that doll? What does the doll mean? Do they have a doll for me? Is this some voodoo thing or something?" I leaned into his shoulder. "Are they going to prick me with needles and kill me?" My body surged alive, searching for any weirdness or pin pricks. He soothed the rising panic, his palm caressing my back.

He forced me away at arm's length. "You trust Jennie, right?" I nodded, my face getting hotter. "She would have told you if they did some sort of weird spell on you. You're fine."

I looked to the starlit sky. He had a good point. "Maybe Courtney did it on her own. Or with Mother. Whoever she is."

"Probably just a goddess that they pray to." Drake pulled me in for a hug again, making me feel like a small child. "I think you're fine. We're going to get to the bottom of this. Do you know where Jennie is right now?"

"No, but I'm sure she wants to talk to us as much as we want to talk to her."

"Good. You find her. I'll go to the cops…without you." He winked. "It'll be better that way."

****

I dropped Drake off at his house to grab his truck and then sped down the mile of the back road to get to Rose's. Lights of a car flashed in my face as I was about to make the turn into my aunt's driveway. The car was nestled across the road right next to the trees. The interior lights came on in the car and Jennie waved.

I pulled the big SUV over and jumped out. The air was brisk and wisps of fog descended low into the fields. My foot caught the lip of the blacktop and I tripped forward, catching myself with my hands on the rough surface. I stood and brushed off the pebbles on my shorts, took another step, and froze.

The roar of an engine accelerated toward me. No lights glinted off the metal of Jennie's car. I turned, and the mass of black, an enormous shape in the horizon, fired straight for me. A horn pierced the silence, blaring a warning. I threw myself backward right before the vehicle flew past. I rolled off the front end of the Escalade and landed half on the blacktop, half on the rocky dirt that lined the road before the fields took over.

My head screamed and my right elbow burst out in fireworks of pain. I rolled to the side and took my elbow in my hand; sticky liquid ran into my palm. The black phantom mass just a shadow in the distance now, still no headlights illuminated the forest and I didn't see marks of red for the taillights.

"Sarah!" Jennie's voice called. The thwack of her flip-flops echoed as they pounded the road. A touch on my shoulder startled me. "Oh my god! Are you okay?"

I moaned and started to cry, a kick-start to my pain, like a gasp after you've choked on something and can't breathe. Big, fat drops ran from my eyes and splashed onto the dirt.

"Ohmygod, ohmygod, ohmygod. That guy tried to hit you!" My head swirled. "Are you hurt? Do you need to go to the hospital?" Jennie paced in front of me and then ran off toward the driveway. "Rose! Rose?!"

I didn't do anything but rock back and forth. Snot and tears running, dripping off the side of my face into a mixed puddle. I squeezed my eyes, saw the shape roaring at me again and cried out. My throat started to hurt. *They didn't even turn around! They didn't even slow down!* The images of my father's accident and my almost accident merged.

My chest expanded and broke repeatedly, wailing into the empty space around me. In between sobs, I heard Jennie talking rapidly. "…this guy…I don't know…he sped up. I honked at him to warn him, but he didn't stop. He went faster. Then Sarah looked up and threw herself backwards. It was so close, so close. It almost hit her! Oh my god! It almost hit her and I almost saw the whole thing!"

Jennie knelt down beside me. Pebbles crunched as Rose approached. A comforting rub warmed the skin on my bicep. I winced and the hand pulled away a little. "Listen to me very carefully, Sarah. Can you hear me?" I nodded, the snot draining into my open mouth. "Are you hurt?" I nodded again. "How bad?"

"I don't know!"

The hand rubbed my arm again. "I need you to calm down so you can tell me. Take a deep breath." I shuddered in a breath. "There you go…let it out now…nice and slow." I repeated the actions my aunt's words demanded, cries slowing, though silent tears still leaked from me. "Now tell me child. Are you hurt?" I winced and nodded my head. "Is anything broken?" I moved my elbow, pulling my palm away from the radiating pain. "Oh dear, you've got a nasty scrape on that elbow." Rose took my hand and peered down. I watched through a kaleidoscope of tears, my aunt's face angular and sometimes blurry. "Jennie, run to the kitchen and wet me some towels." Jennie's quick retreating footsteps padded the grass. "How's your head?"

I took stock. I could still think clear enough. It hurt, pounded even, but I didn't feel I was in any imminent danger. "I think it's okay."

Rose smoothed back the hair from my face. "Dear, dear, so you *can* talk?" I tried to smile. "Do you think you can get up?" Rose held out a hand and I rolled to my back, grabbing it with the arm that didn't take the full brunt of the fall. Rose tugged and I got up on shaky legs. With an arm around my waist, Rose led me back to the big house.

Halfway, Jennie met us and a cool cloth swathed my elbow. "Thanks, Jennie."

"Are you okay?" Her voice was frightened. It was like nothing I'd ever heard her sound like before. It was tiny, sad, not the usual ass-kicking attitude she liked to put on.

I nodded. "Think so." I forced a smile to my lips.

In the kitchen, Jennie and Rose worked to freshen me up. Rose said the injuries weren't too bad. "A bump to the noggin and a scrape on the elbow. Lucky."

Jennie agreed and when she went to recount what happened, Rose silenced her with a warning stare. Jennie's mouth slammed shut in mid-sentence. "If you want, Jennie can walk you up to your room, but then she has to go. You need some rest."

"Yeah, that'd be nice."

Jennie took me by the good hand and we headed for the stairs. Rose moved into our path. "Next time, don't be where you shouldn't be." She smiled and placed a soft kiss on my cheek. "I don't want to have to worry about you when I've got so many other things going on."

I nodded and allowed Jennie to lead me away. "Jeez, weird much?"

"Huh?"

"Your aunt," Jennie whispered as we walked slowly up the stairs.

I shrugged. "Didn't notice." I winced as we passed by the railing, my hurt elbow skimming against the wood.

Jennie opened the door to my room and turned the lights on before we went in. "Do you want to call Drake? I see you guys are really getting close." Jennie smiled as she helped me into bed.

I reached around to my pocket and groaned. "Ugh, my phone."

"What?"

"It was in my pocket when I fell. Can you get it out for me?"

I twisted and Jennie reached into my pocket and brought out the cell phone. If that's what you would call it now, considering it was broke to hell. The screen was smashed and we couldn't even get it to turn on.

A voice called up the stairs. "Time to go now, Jennie."

Jennie looked toward the hallway and then back to me. "What's his number? I'll call him from my phone."

"I don't know. It was in my cell." I threw the dilapidated phone onto the quilt and it bounced off and crashed onto the floor.

Jennie's eyes followed it. "Alrighty then. I'll call when I get home. I'm sure his number is in the phonebook or something."

"Thanks."

Jennie turned and walked toward the door, then stopped and spun around. "Can I see you tomorrow? We have lots to discuss."

I sighed mentally. As if I didn't already have enough to worry about. Now I had to recover from almost being run over, like my dad. *Like my...dad.* "Do you think this...?" I motioned to my body. "...is related to that?" I jabbed my thumb in the direction of the window and hopefully pointed to somewhere in the vicinity of the clearing.

"Yes, I do, Sarah." Jennie lifted her shirt and brought out her Wicca handbook. "Here. You're going to need this."

****

Ten minutes later, the phone rang. This time, I didn't have the strength to creep down the stairs and listen in on the conversation. I knew it was Drake, though Rose never came up the stairs with the phone. *I guess a hurt, pathetic girl with a target on her back doesn't get to have phone calls.*

Chapter Twenty-Six

1639

"Come!" Two men descended the steps. Isabella wrapped herself in her arms. She did not look up. She did not want to see who came for her. A hand pulled at her sleeve and she resisted only for a moment before remembering the blow of the judge's palm into Mrs. Shipton's face. She allowed the magistrate to move her, but her strength and her senses gave him nothing. He twirled her around like a puppet, holding her, making sure she stood on two feet and dragged her when she did not. "Help me, you fools. She is too weak to stand on her own."

The two men hesitated, so Magistrate Ludington grabbed hold of her hands and pulled. It knocked Isabella to the floor and he dragged her unmoving body across the damp dirt. Her back hit into the stair and her feet thudded every time they landed on a new step. He grunted at her weight, heaving her up until she lay completely flat on her back. She opened her eyes and saw the moon and the stars. A single tear leaked out before she shut them again.

Hard footsteps raced up the stairs, and Mrs. Shipton began to scream. Two men halted her, grabbing her shoulders. "Stop," Mr. Ludington ordered. "I want her to watch. Then she can see what she is about next."

The pathetic woman dropped to her knees. "Oh no, please. Please, no."

Isabella opened her eyes and looked around. A crowd gathered in a circle around her. Men, women, and children she all knew by name. They used to stop to talk with her before the weather changed, and the crops failed, and the witches were found. Before this, they were neighbors and friends. They were nice and agreeable. Now, they stood over her, repulsed, angry, mouths tight and eyes folded and leveled at her.

A rumble started from the back. "Witch!" someone called. Isabella winced.

"Blasphemer."

"Die you unholy creature."

"May Satan save you now!" Mrs. Ludington screeched before pelting her with a handful of stones. Isabella shut her eyes, flinching away. Two more men broke the circle and carried a trunk of an old pine and laid it next to her.

Mr. Ludington hauled her up by the shoulders and propped her next to the dead tree. "You two, tie her up." Limp Isabella stilled, her heart frozen on a single beat. No one moved toward her. "Thomas…Tie. Her. Up."

"What about her trial?" Mrs. Shipton screamed.

"Silence!" Isabella winced at the sharp cry from Magistrate Ludington. "There will be no trial. Evidences in this instance were plenty. Isabella Lynne has been seen in the woods at night, not only once, not only twice, but on numerous occasions. We found ingredients for her potions. She bewitched my son! We will not honor the direct descendant of Satan with a trial."

Feet shuffled toward her and she squeezed her eyes tight, not wanting to see Thomas. She did not want to cry out. She did not want to whimper or whine. If she were to see him, she would do all of them at once. Instead, she tried to grasp hold of the memory of his face when they stole the kiss in her room, or when he met her in the barn for the first time. Surely their love was not blasphemous.

Thomas. Her Thomas.

She wondered which hands that touched her were his. They were both rough, forcing her arms behind her, the rope dug into the flesh of her wrists and burned as it tugged across her. Then came her feet. The rope snaked in and out, around her ankles and the log and as it pulled tighter, she clenched her teeth to drown out a cry.

None of her body lay on the ground anymore. It suspended in air, her head slightly higher than her feet and she moved now, jostled about on the rounded log. The knots of the rope held her tight. It gave her no room to move her wrists or ankles. If she were to think about escape, hope for escape, it was not possible. The journey was short, her head knocked against the wood as they swung her up. She fell forward slightly, only as much room as her arms gave her. Her shoulders seared in pain as the weight of her body hung against it.

She tried to bend her knees to release the pressure, but it did not work. Her eyes firmly shut, she flinched as objects struck her. Some pierced her skin, others bounced off and left bolts of pain flowing through her. More cries of "Witch!" yelled out until the entire village seemed to shout at once.

"Villagers of Adams, I, your magistrate, have done it again! We will burn away the evil that inflicts this town. We will make this right again. We will feed your children's mouths. We will survive!" The pillar of the trunk swayed back and forth. "We must rid our town of evil to do it! And right now, two such evils will be burned!"

Two?

Cheers and chants of "Die witches" sounded from every corner of the little town square. Isabella's eyes popped open. She looked to her right. Nothing. She looked to her left.

There she stared into eyes. Familiar brown eyes. Brown eyes that turned down with sorrow when she was a little girl and scraped her knee or ruined a dress. Brown eyes that smiled at her when she helped with chores. Brown eyes that mirrored the flames below as the hay beneath them caught fire.

Her mother's eyes.

Chapter Twenty-Seven

Present Day

"Where do you think you're going?"

I halted as I discreetly, or so I thought, descended the stairs. Rose came into the foyer, checking her wristwatch. It was five or so. She had already hindered all my attempts to get out of the house to meet Drake and Jennie. Every moment counted though. I didn't care if my body wasn't in top shape. I needed to be out there, seeing who killed my father and who wanted to kill me. "I've got to see Drake. It's important."

"I don't think that's a good idea. You banged your head last night. You're not going anywhere."

"But Rose—"

"No buts." Her eyebrow shot in the air.

"I really need to see him. Can he come over?"

"He could if he tried honey, but he hasn't."

I sighed. *Yeah, I noticed.* Neither of them tried to come over, even though Jennie said she would. "Can I call him then?"

"You don't want to seem clingy, do you?" Rose stopped at the bottom of the stairs. "I know him and that Marlene girl were really close. She wasn't clingy. She's a free spirit." She huffed and put her hands on her hips. "We all thought he'd end up with her just…"

"Just what?"

"It didn't…click…I guess."

I smiled, not feeling particularly happy. I didn't like where this conversation was headed. "Good for me then."

"Actually, Honey," Rose said, frowning, "I think I should tell you. Before you showed up, I'm pretty sure they were going to get back together."

My heart freefell to the ground. "That would explain why she hates me."

"Probably." Rose giggled. The sound quickly turned eerie, like a Halloween clown's maniacal laugh. "Once you've gone, I'm sure things will go back to as if you were never here."

A fire sparked to life in my belly. "Drake says he's not interested in her."

Rose shrugged. "I'm just telling you an old wise woman's point of view. Take it as you wish." She waved her hands and walked into her bedroom.

I might have taken her advice if I hadn't pored through Jennie's Wiccan handbook all day, devouring the information. And I still might have listened, except I came across a picture of a doll within the pages. Marlene's doll. A binding doll.

I ignored my aunt and walked to the front door. I pulled it open, smiling, and walked through. After easing the door shut, I ran to the SUV, hands already pulling at the keys I found on the side table from my pocket. *One thing the old wise woman doesn't know: how to live with a teenager.*

I started the car and gunned it for the main road. My tires threw rocks into the grass as I took a right toward Drake's house. I got to the old, country farm in no time, religiously checking the rearview mirror for Rose following in her own car, shaking her finger at me and saying what a naughty girl I was.

I pulled up to Drake's farmhouse. The front curtains moved and his face came into view. I jumped from the car, but a head rush knocked me off kilter so I stood still, gripping the door handle for balance before Drake rushed over to envelop me in a hug.

"Are you okay? I've been calling you all day."

"My cell's dead, smashed."

"No, I know. I called the house phone."

"It hasn't rung all day." I smacked the door with my fist. "Aunt Rose must have turned the ringer off."

"So are you alright?" He hugged me again, squeezing me. His grip moved to my hurt elbow and I moaned. He broke away and studied my injuries, turning my hand over in his. "Nasty."

"Yeah, battle scar, I guess." Drake frowned, letting my hand drop. His face turned chastising, like he was sick of having to remind me of something I did wrong over and over again. "Someone tried to run me over," I started. "This has everything to do with my dad and this crazy town. What are we gonna do?"

"Not you too," Drake groaned.

"What?"

"Jennie's been ringing my phone off the hook. She's convinced these things are related."

"How can they not be?"

"Someone didn't try to run you over. Those things just don't happen in this town."

"They did. Hello. Look at my dad." Drake sighed and my nerves frayed at the already worn edges. "Jesus, Drake, your feelings are giving me whiplash. Do you believe that what is happening is happening or not? Did you not see what happened to Marlene yesterday?"

"Yeah, I did, and I talked to Marlene. She was invited to the meeting, she just showed up late." Drake laughed. "You see, Sarah? There are always rational explanations for things."

"What? About what they did at the meeting? That doll is a binding doll. It—"

Drake waved me away. "Some weird Wiccan stuff. God, I think you should stay out of it. Jennie kept talking about some crap that happened hundreds of years ago. I mean, really?"

I pulled away from him. "This is crazy. I mean, one minute you're right there with me, and now the next, after I practically get run over, the biggest clue of all, and you think this is all some misunderstanding?"

Drake grabbed me by the shoulders. "You need to stop getting involved. Nothing is going on here. We're in Adams, Virginia for Christ's sake. I think there are only two hundred people living here. Nothing is going on. You need to stop prying."

I shrugged him off. "Just…whatever, okay." I fiddled with the keys in my hands. "I'm gonna go."

"Just because I think you're wrong about this town doesn't mean I want you to leave. Sarah." He grabbed for me again, eyes boring into me, filling me with a yearning so bad it made me want to fall into his arms. His body radiated need and like the pull of gravity, I was swept away. "I really want to kiss you right now." His eyes lightened. "Come on." He reached for me and I nudged my foot forward. "I don't want to worry about some conspiracy theory. I want to spend a fun summer with you."

He leaned into me, kissing me with all our desires laid bare before us. He kissed the worry out of me, the tense headache and rigid bones. He wound his hands in my hair, pressing my lips to his so hotly, so intimately that if I watched two people doing this on the street, I would blush immediately for watching something so personal, so raw.

"Is that all you got?"

I jumped and snatched my head away. The kiss ended badly. Part of my lip was probably stuck to one of

Drake's teeth. I spun, heart hammering away in my chest with a chisel. The inside of my mouth tasted metallic.

"Huh? Is that all you got, Mother?"

"Jennie?" I found her, face shaking and cheeks flaming red. "What are you—?"

"Get in your truck now, Sarah. I'll explain on the way."

"But—"

"Now!" I didn't budge. "Trust me." Jennie shook something on the ground in front of her from a canister. "Get behind this line." Frozen, my feet were planted into the earth like a cypress tree, and my fingers were roots that intertwined with Drake's. I didn't know if I could go anywhere even if I wanted to.

"Please," Drake scoffed. "I told you this girl was crazy."

"Sarah…" Jennie's voice turned to buzzing alarm. "I believe you. I believe everything you've said and I know why. I know everything and I'll tell you. Just get behind this line and we'll drive away from here."

I scooted a few inches away from Drake, dropping his heavy hand. He stared down at my feet, blinking, like he thought he imagined I moved away from him. "You can't be serious, Sarah. I told you. There's nothing going on here."

"Don't listen to him anymore. He—"

"He thinks he's in love with you is what he is." Drake peered at me with half-lidded eyes, unscathed, innocent baby-like eyes. "God Sarah, I've been trying to hold back because you were so unsure. You've got a lot going on. Your dad, your mom, meeting your aunt for the first time. But come on. From the first time I saw you, we clicked." He reached for me, and it wasn't just a hand reaching out, it was like two hearts melting to one. My uncertainty washed away in a tide of emotions freed after a surge of tsunamis happily broke my broken heart.

Someone loved me. Someone wanted to spend time with me. I couldn't remember feeling this way…like, ever. My dad wrote about it in his journal. Wrote how great of a family we were. I never got to experience a tight family unit though. Mom was always off trying to pick up a new step-dad to make us a whole family, never realizing what I needed was her. Just her. A mom to make me feel whole. A family tree that didn't matter if it was only a two-person deal, it was still complete and real.

I reached out to Drake, a tear running down my face. He smiled at me, one lip higher than the other and those cute, tiny lines creased his mouth.

A sting flared on the back of my calf. Tiny beads pelted me from behind on my bare arms and legs. Some struck Drake in the face. He shook his head. "What the…what's going on?"

"Drake?" The question dropped from my lips like lead. I didn't know what to ask him. I needed everything from him and I wasn't quite sure how to ask him for everything. It was like asking someone for a rainbow or a star.

What should I do? Did he really mean he loved me? There were so many endings and not enough time.

Jennie ran forward and grasped me by the elbow. "Get in the car!" It screamed in pain. She dragged me back and pushed me toward the passenger seat. Drake stood sullenly, looking after us, his mouth pulled down into a frown, face smeared in confusing pain.

Off to the right, movement caught my eye. Rose emerged from the cornfield. Nothing touched the green plants, nothing moved them from her way, but the stalks parted for her like a countrified automatic door. So unnatural, like nails scraping something so hard you cringe, or knees folding in the wrong direction that your body moves in revulsion.

"Oh, fuck. Get in the car!" Jennie pushed me so hard that I fell into the open door. I hopped onto the seat and a couple seconds later, Jennie jumped in, turning the car over too hard that the engine squealed in protest. "Shut the door!"

"Drake? What about Drake?"

"Shut the door!" Jennie put the car in drive and slammed on the gas. A cloud of dirt swirled around the vehicle. I pulled the door shut and peered out the window.

Drake and Rose stood together. The older woman's hand around his shoulders as she comforted him.

"You better start talking."

"I knew you would come here first. Why? I told you I needed to talk to you."

"What are you talking about? I haven't talked to you all day. I haven't talked to *anybody* all day."

"I talked to you on the phone."

"Hello. Did you not just hear me? Nobody called me all day. Nobody. The only person I've talked to is Rose."

"Shit!" Jennie banged her hands against the steering wheel. "It's worse than I thought."

"What?"

She spoke to the air. "Oh my god. She can transfigure."

"Transfigure?" Mentally, I scanned the pages of Jennie's book. The name sparked something, but it couldn't be.

"Yes. She can make herself whoever she wants."

I saw the picture in the book now, an ugly, warted hag turning into a beautiful woman with the figure of a dancer. "Body or voice?" The script said something about there being a difference. "You only heard her voice, well, my voice." Jennie's face turned cockeyed, unbalanced, a ghastly awe. I didn't know if she was terrified, or if I had shocked her with my black magic knowledge. "I've been reading your Wiccan Handbook," I clarified.

"I don't know. Maybe both?" Jennie steered the SUV around a sharp corner, it tittered on its wheels. "Both would be bad. Really bad. We wouldn't know who she was or wasn't."

"You're sure? Absolutely sure it's my aunt?"

"Positive. Did you not notice the freakin' corn? Hello?"

"This is not happening." I clenched the dash in front of me. "Why her? Why?"

"Think about it. It may not *be* her." My face pinched together as I shot her a look. "She can transfigure, take over bodies. I know everything." Her voice came out low, hypnotic.

"What do you know? Tell me."

"Gladly." Jennie rounded another corner again, a less severe one that only sent the SUV's tires screeching against the pavement. "You know that journal we found in your aunt's library?"

"Uh huh."

"Well…I read it. I pulled your car into the driveway before I left last night and I saw it on the passenger seat from the other day. I figured since you were…incapacitated, you'd want me to do some snooping."

I rolled my hand over. "So…"

"So I know what's happening. The journal belonged to this girl named Isabella who lived here a freaking long time ago. She was in love with this guy named Thomas—"

Scenery blipped by like seconds on a timer. "Please, Jennie. Get to the important part." I didn't want to know what happened when it blinked zero.

"I *am* at the important part. His father didn't approve and mysteriously she was convicted of witchcraft and burned on the stake. She was one of the witches burned here."

"Okay…and this has to do with me because…"

"Because the symbol we've both seen is in her journal. It isn't the sign for the devil. It was a sign of a local family, the Shipton's." I sighed, about to open my mouth to tell Jennie to get to the freakin' point already when she rushed out, "Mother Shipton to be exact."

"Mother? The one you guys conjured in the ceremony yesterday night?"

Face pasty white and voice hollowed out, Jennie said, "I didn't know, Sarah. Really, I didn't. There's something else. Something worse." Jennie squirmed in the leather seat. "She put a curse on the family that killed Isabella. Drake is a direct descendant of that family. I went to the library first thing this morning and looked it up. Thomas Ludington's family tree reaches all the way to the Connors. They changed their name sometime after the witch was burnt here. Tried to hide. There are local conspiracy books filled with the mysterious curse at the library." She pounded the dash. "I tried to get Drake all day. I tried. Your aunt got to him first."

My stomach jittered in an ugly roil of acid as I ran a shaky hand through my hair, processing everything. The Ludington's. The name wasn't unfamiliar. I read it on Drake's family tree, on the canvas above the mantle pictures of his lost loved ones. The loved ones he lost from this curse.

I finally understood the infatuation Rose had with Drake now and his grandfather's reluctance to say anything. She needed to keep them close. I studied the double yellow line as it whisked underneath the Escalade at seventy miles per hour. "Where are we going?"

"They know we know. Something needs to happen or we'll end up like your dad."

I pressed a hand over my mouth. Fantasized movie pictures flashed in front of me of what my father described my life to be like. Me with my mother, sliding at playgrounds and baking together. Smiling at one another like in those corny Hallmark cards.

My body stiffened. Drake had had that too once. She took it away. She took it away from both of us. "I don't know about you, but I think we need to get the bitch."

Chapter Twenty-Eight

1639

Thomas stood off to the side, next to his father. The elder Ludington held a firm hand around his son's waist.

"Prepare the other."

Thomas hesitated. If he stepped to move, would his knee would buckle beneath him, send him falling to the dirt in the town square? Would everyone notice then? Would they realize Thomas Ludington just stood by and watched his love burn?

His father explained before that his feelings were not his own. The conniving witch made him feel. Made him love her, sin for her. He was supposed to feel this. He would ache for her like any other lost love. Mourn her as if she did not influence his heart.

"Son, it is time now." The magistrate released his hold. Thomas still stood so he took a silent step toward Mother Shipton, the third witch to burn tonight. He walked steady, relieved to feel his limbs working correctly though his heart and head were a different matter. With each step toward the devil's daughter, his heart splintered and his head clouded in an angry fog.

Thomas stalked up next to a large mess, a shuddering knot of clothes. He kicked her. The toe of his boot glanced off the woman's shoulder. "It is time," he mimicked his father's words.

Mrs. Shipton lifted her shaking face. A pool of tears flooded her eyes and ran over. Her wrinkled skin caught the clear water and funneled it through the deep grooves. "You do not know what you have done." Her lips, cracked with thirst, trembled. Thomas signaled the two men waiting with the next spire. She turned her head, her eyes picking up the men carrying the log. She tossed her head back and forth, and her brown hair, laced with wiry silver strands, tangled itself on her wet cheeks. "I tried to tell you. I did. Your love was not a witch. She burned an innocent." Mrs. Shipton gathered herself up and stood eye-to-eye with Thomas. He waved away her guards who reached out to restrain her. "Your father made me do it. He used me. He did not want you to marry her."

Mr. Austen and Mr. Leigh balanced the heavy wood beam next to Thomas, one end in the dirt, the other angling off toward the darkening night. Mr. Leigh handed him the rope. The guards dragged the witch to the log as the other men held it steady, waiting for the weight of the woman to bear on it.

Thomas interlaced the rope around the old woman's feet, winding the coarse cord about the wood and flesh, pulling and tugging the wiry rough against the witch's skin. He cared not if he marred the hag's old wrinkles, not like he did with Isabella. When he wound the rope around Mrs. Shipton's waist and hands, she whispered to him, "You know why they call me Mother, do not you?" A taunting smile played across her lips. "I gave her the dreams. With her…and me. I have powers. Ancient powers. He thought if I scared her she would stop seeing you." She giggled; Thomas tightened the knot around her wrists. "He did not realize your feelings were true. You loved her. You loved one another."

Thomas lingered over the last knot. "Then when you came to him and wanted him to sanction your marriage, he lost it. He had to take care of her." Thomas' mouth slacked. "You are wondering how I know all this?" She bit down on her lip. The rope cut through flesh. The spire jostled as the men stepped toward the waiting crowd. "Your father is watching me as you did your Isabella." Mrs. Shipton laughed, pitch rising as they carried her further away. "Except he knows I am a witch. I partnered with evil some time ago to get my powers. You only thought your love was lost to the devil. She was not."

Thomas staggered forward, following after the mad laughter. "Why?" he choked out, but his words were smothered silent by his father's booming voice, listing the accusations as Mrs. Shipton swayed above the villagers. Her spire found a place to rest in the hole next to the other two.

A thick, black smoke hovered in wisps amongst the crowd. Spots of dark gray clouds still billowed from the ashes, rising in the air.

"Do you have any last words?"

The wind shifted. A gray veil crossed in front of the hanging witch. The torch man waited on the cusp of the brittle hay and browned grass.

"You stare at me. Mock me. Curse me." Mother Shipton leveled her eyes at her fellow neighbors. They glanced away or down at their dusty shoes. No one screamed out as was done with the Lynnes. No one threw stones or stared hard. They cowered under her gaze, the dark stare of power. "But you shall not forget me." She turned toward the magistrate and mirrored his proud head, chin high and straight faced. "The honored line shall perish, starting with the two."

The judge ran to the torch man. "Throw it on. She speaks her evil."

The man dropped the torch, hands flying to his ears. The crowd followed, scattering and running in a tangled spider web to their homes. Cries rang out and rose up to the night. Men clung to their wives, tugged at their dresses as they scampered to their homes.

Mother Shipton's laughter rang, a yell in a pack of whispers. "The ones they hold as fairest, for their loves anew. A curse to bind them." The magistrate bent over, found the still flaming torch in the sand and threw it at the witch. "For me to find them." The torch hit the witch's waist and fell to the dry hay. Fire immediately caught and spread. Her eyes stared at the rising flames and then moved to catch the cold, unyielding glare of her lover.

"And I will do as you have done to me."

****

Thomas waited until after they removed the Lynne women's belongings from their cottage. He searched and found nothing but Isabella's journals in his sack. His father insisted on keeping the desk and the journals, which he thought odd. *Was not it always imperative to burn the witch's belongings as well as the witch?*

They sat at the dinner table. Betrayal pulsed through him, but he doubted his father noticed. He set down his spoon and cleared his throat. "Father. I must know."

Magistrate Ludington threw his spoon to the table. "Know what?"

"Was Isabella a witch?"

"You doubt me?"

"Mother Shipton said you were lovers. You and her. She said you made her do things to Isabella."

"Witches, witches, they are all witches!" He stood, mouth still open from his sudden surge, then his eyes widened and he began to claw at his throat. The veins in his neck protruded.

"Father?"

The man fell to the floor. Thomas pushed the chairs away and stood over, shaking his limp form.

Footsteps strode into the room. Thomas looked up. His mother stood there, hands entwined around her middle, a sly smile covered her face. A flash of the old witch pierced his mind and for a moment, he did not stare at his mother, but at Mrs. Shipton.

"You are next."

ERIN BUTLER

Chapter Twenty-Nine

Present Day

"A hardware store? Seriously?" I flattened myself against the seat as Jennie ran over a curb in front of a shop just outside Adams.

"It's a Country Store. We need some things if we're going to save the whole damn town."

"Don't you have powers or something? Can't you do something?"

"That's why we're here. I need some...tools."

"Like wrenches and screwdrivers?"

Jennie shot me a death look. "No princess, like rope...and a doll. I'm going to try and make a binding doll to hopefully undo the hold she has over everyone. Oh." Jennie jacked her thumb in the direction of the backseat. "And I need more salt."

I twisted in the seat and found a canister clearly labeled salt surrounded by white granules. "I knew they made the doll for Marlene. I read it in your book." I turned forward again. "I just don't get the salt."

"You must not have read everything then." The SUV jerked and came to a stop right in front of the shop, in the fire lane. Jennie jumped out, leaving the key in the ignition, the car running. I hesitated. "It'll be fine," she shouted as she banged the hood, jarring me to attention.

Inside the store, Jennie continued in whispers, "Salt is a very basic negation spell, protective." I stalked next to her, feeling pretty stupid. "You ever watch football?" Jennie sighed.

"Well, yeah."

"Think of salt as the protective pads the player wears. As long as you got some on, it won't hurt."

Voice tired, I asked, "What's the plan?"

"We need to get my tools and head to Heritage Park."

"Heritage Park? Where everybody and their mother is right now? That sounds like a horrible idea."

Jennie's jaw tightened, leaving her face angular. "If you were to see a layout of the park, you'd notice the inside is in the shape of a pentagram. We usually hold our coven meetings there. Of course, with Settler's Days, we had to move temporarily." She peeked at me and noticing I was still following, she continued, "It's the most magic filled place in Adams. My powers alone won't be enough. I need to be there."

"The park is in the shape of a pentagram? And nobody thinks this is weird?"

"It's Adams."

I peeked up and down the aisles filled with wheelbarrows, bird feed, garden tools, and everything else country. "So? It's Adams, not some city in hell."

"I don't know. It looks pretty?"

The park was pretty and I wouldn't have realized it was shaped like that if Jennie hadn't said anything. "Okay, so if it's the most powerful place in Adams, don't you think Rose is going to want to use that to her advantage too?"

Jennie's eyes flicked from one aisle to the next. "Yes."

I put my hand out on Jennie's shoulder and stopped her. "She already has been using it. Oh my god, I'm so stupid." My mind flicked back to every time I thought the Crazies were acting, well, crazy. People spacing out, repeating their words. I scanned the aisle signs. "We're going to need lots of salt."

Jennie smirked. We grabbed a cart and started to load up. Jennie picked a rope off the shelf, a doll in the clearance aisle, and I leveled my hand across the shelf where they stored the water softener salt. They crashed into the cart one-by-one. The old geezer shoppers shook their heads at me and kept glancing back out of the corners of their eyes.

We stood in line. A short guy with a god complex rang up items. He flirted with the old ladies in front of us and once he started scanning our items, he pulled out his shockingly white teeth and dumbo grin. "How are you two beauties doing today?"

I snatched the plastic bags from his hands and Jennie tapped her foot against the concrete floor. The movement didn't faze him. Jennie shook her hair around so it fell in her face and she pouted her lower lip.

His face lit. "That'll be 25.32."

My mouth dropped and I glanced at Jennie, her hands unconsciously felt for her purse. Of course, she didn't have it on her and neither did I. I didn't think I'd need my wallet. Didn't think I'd be shopping at the hardware-slash-magical shop today, make that shoplifting at the hardware-slash-magical shop today.

Jennie didn't lose a beat. She made a show of patting her back pockets and then dropped her mouth with her pouty lip and exclaimed, "Oh man. I forgot the money our mom gave us in the car. Can we run out and bring it back to you?"

The boy's eyebrow twitched. "Sure," he said cheerfully, leaning in toward Jennie. "As long as you bring me back a piece of paper with your number on it."

"Will do," she said, winking at him.

I steered the cart toward the exit. "What are—?"

"Shh." Once we got outside, Jennie ran to the running car and started shoveling items into the backseat. "Get in the driver's seat and get ready."

I ran to the driver's side door and watched Jennie shovel handfuls of salt into the SUV, her eyes teetering back and forth between the task and the main door. "Oh sh—"

"What?"

"Get in the car. Now."

"Hey, do you need help?" the checkout boy called to her, wringing his hands in his green Country Store smock.

Jennie dropped the canisters of salt she had in her hands, somehow managed to shove the cart away, close the door, and hop in the front seat all before the boy knew anything was wrong.

"Hey–hey—"

I peeled out, scaring a young couple so bad they fell back on their butts as I maneuvered around them. The rearview mirror revealed three very pissed off faces. I cringed and sunk my fingernails into the leather of the steering wheel.

"It's okay," Jennie said, pulling her hair behind her ears. "It's emergency circumstances."

I eased my grip and concentrated on the road. I'd never been down these before, only sticking to the main highways on my way up here and then the tiny side streets of Adams.

Jennie reached behind her seat and grabbed the doll. It was an old one with tan fabric skin and yellow yarn for hair. It had blue eyes and a cute little nose sewn into it. Jennie stripped the doll of its jean skirt and doggie shirt. "Is that going to work?" I asked.

"I don't see why not."

"Okay, so I'll pull up to Heritage Park, we get out and what? We just walk up?"

Jennie nonchalantly petted the doll's hair, her face expressionless as she stared ahead. "Yup. That's what we do." She switched her gaze to the doll. "Then we kneel in the middle, before the stage, and—"

"Wait. *We* kneel in the middle?"

Jennie nodded. "I can't do it without you. I need your energy."

"But I'm not a psychic, or a Wiccan either."

"Doesn't make a difference. I just need you to concentrate and repeat after me."

Drake flashed into my mind, that solemn, hollow expression. It was him, but not really him. "I can do that."

When we pulled into a parking spot near Heritage Park, the first person I recognized was Courtney, the high priestess. "Do you think she's in on it?"

Jennie shook her head. "Nah, it's all Mother."

"She's controlling everybody? Drake?"

"Everybody."

I turned to face Jennie in the seat, her face tight, unbreakable stone. "Let's do this."

I left the Escalade running in a parking space near the statue of the first settler in case we needed to make another quick escape. The statue's eyes called out to me again and my gaze traveled down the length of the statue to the C.

Of course. C for Connors. The Crazies were changing the settler's last name from Ludington to Connors.

I marched through the park to catch up with Jennie, holding a couple of plastic bags brimming with salt canisters. Jennie held the rope and the doll.

No one bothered us as we walked toward the center of the park, nor did I see any more coven members. Yet.

People, almost imperceptibly, moved out of the way when we walked through. A few slid just out of reach as we stalked on and a couple even completely turned directions when they saw us coming. Pretty soon, a clear, straight shot to the stage bloomed out before us.

I quickened my pace and heard the rubber squish of Jennie's shoes right next to me. "Is right here okay?" I asked when I found what I thought to be the middle. I scanned the park, calculating distances and from every point, I felt we had the right place. "Jennie?"

I spun and landed on Jennie's blanched, unfeeling face. "Mother controls everybody, Sarah," Jennie's distracted voice wafted to me.

The doll and the rope fell from her grasp and landed on the green grass. My face folded and a string tugged in my stomach. Mother's using the power of the park right now.

Jennie lifted a hand. Her wrist tugged taut, though her fingers limped from the rest of her arm like free strings. I slowly turned in that direction and gasped. My heart jarred inside me, screeching to a halt.

Right off the center of the stage, my mother descended from a makeshift cross, her body falling forward like the lifeless dummy days ago. Her eyes were shut, no other telling signs proved she lived. That she still breathed life in her.

Chapter Thirty

Present Day

I staggered forward even before my legs felt any pressure and then I started to jog. I needed to get to Mom.

My nose crunched as I slammed into something, but there was nothing. Absolutely nothing in front of me. I brought a hand to my nose as droplets of blood dripped into my palms. I wiped my hands off on my jeans and stretched them out into the space ahead of me.

It was just like the library. I rotated in every direction, reaching out, and an invisible hard surface met my searching hands all the way around. I dipped my shoulder low and banged into the wall. The force didn't give, didn't even groan, or reveal any evidence that what I did helped. I spread my palms out, pressed my forehead against the clear, solid air, and peered at my mom.

A thump sounded around the whole park, as well as the echo of the reverberation off the downtown buildings. My mom blinked until her eyes popped open, fear making them twitch as she took in her surroundings. Townspeople rustled by her, uncaring, as if she too, was invisible.

"Ex-excuse me?" My head snapped up as I heard the familiar voice. I looked around at the people moving past her. *Oh. My. God.* Mom was mic'd. I could hear everything she was saying. "Excuse me. I'm looking for my daughter."

I lurched backward and bounced off the wall. "Jennie, it's my mom." I turned and found Jennie still standing, unchanged. "Jennie!" I banged my fist against the wall. "It's my mom. Help her."

Pictures blinked in my mind of Mom leaving the house with guys as she waved to me in my bedroom window, and showing up late to school concerts, shyly excusing herself as she bumped every other parent's leg on her way to the lone empty seat in the middle. It was always that one empty seat in the middle, never a side seat, an aisle seat. And here again, my mother transcended the norm, elevated in the air in front of the whole dang town. "Jennie." I broke down, tears streaming from my eyes. "Please. It's my mom. My mom. Help her."

The townspeople gathered around, forming a semi-circle. I was in the middle and Cici was at the front. They pushed back even more, creating a wide girth around us.

My mom found me now and she broke down in tears, which was so not like her. She tugged on her wrists, cries echoing, bouncing around the park. "Sarah, I came to get you. I came to get you," she repeated.

Behind her, Rose crept out on stage. My aunt, possessed by a witch, marched right to the end of the stage. The crowd ballooned out even more, eyes transfixed on her. She clapped her hands and bounced up and down on her toes. "Ha, this is so perfect," she squealed.

The crowd applauded. Cici's heels dug into the wood, scraping against the cross as she tried to back up. I turned to face the crowd. Their faces lit up in excitement, a sneering grin passing from one to the other. Fathers lifted their tots on their shoulders so they could see better. Little kids pulled at their mothers' arms while they hopped up and down. They acted like little fan girls in the face of a celebrity.

My belly churned, an eggbeater tossing around the insides. I bent at the waist to throw up. Some of the liquid stained the invisible wall. A toddler close to me laughed and pointed, tugging her mother's dress with her free hand.

She controls everybody. And I mean everybody. She's using the power of the pentagram like we wanted to. She's making them all stare at this as if they want it.

"Perfect," Mother echoed again. "We'll have a little appetizer before our dessert." The old woman in my aunt's body glanced to the side of the stage where two men in brown trousers held Marlene. Drake stood next to them, reaching out to Marlene, his face contorted in agony. "Thomas and his beloved, Isabella."

"Nooo!" I cried out. I wanted to throw up my entire stomach, I really did. I wanted to feel my blood surge for that one, tiny second before splattering on the grass.

Mother turned her head slow until it landed on me. It tilted to the side, then righted itself, standing square on her shoulders. "No? Who did you think it was, you? Ha," she laughed. She bounced on her toes again, a kindergartener at her school birthday party. "It was never you, Sarah. It's always been Isabella." She cupped her hand in front of her mouth and whispered like we weren't surrounded by a hundred people. "Well, Marlene." Her voice sounded raspy, cracking as it came through the speakers. "It could have been you. I even tried to make it you. You just wouldn't give the thought of your father up. Damn. Your persistence really pissed me off. Then, you couldn't even get run over correctly."

My mouth dropped. The witch hardly noticed. She started speaking again. "Look at him." She pointed to Drake. I shook my head, nose stinging from the jagged movements. "Look at him!" she screamed.

The speakers shrieked. I plugged my ears until the echo died before peeking over. Drake knelt before

Marlene, shoulders heaving, his hands covering his face. I shook my head in disbelief. "Not possible." *He loves me. He told me he loved me.*

"I'm a witch. I can make the impossible, possible. I have..." She shrugged her shoulders like it was no big deal. "...powers." She peered down at herself and grabbed the cotton of her frumpy dress. "Of course, I prefer the younger bodies. Unfortunately, Drake's bitch of a mother had other plans and I had to make do."

A warrior growl punctured the buzzing speaker silence and a rock pelted Mother in the head. She fell to her knees, her face flickering between her borrowed body and an old, haggard, sallow face with hateful eyes.

Drake's grandfather ran forth from the crowd and pelted her again with a big, black stone. Mother covered herself and the rock bounced off her forearm, falling to the feet of Cici's pyre.

My mother shied away from the man, twisting, her arm bending in unnatural angles. I yelled to her, "It's okay, Mom." My voice didn't reach her, though. The reassurance fell empty in the expanse between us. I didn't have a mic like the others.

Drake's grandfather, relieved of all the rocks he'd stored in the crook of his arms, stood before the stage, hands empty now as they fell to his sides. His shoulders slumped forward, shaking. "You killed them. You killed them all."

Mother stood, really pissed now, her face entirely mutated into the unknown one, who I would have guessed for everything was Mother Shipton. "You know I did."

"What did you do to Drake?" Mr. Connors' voice broke and cracked.

"There is no Drake. That's Thomas. And I think you know what happened to Thomas. He made a decision. It was wrong. He had to be punished."

"No, Drake is real. Turn him back. He's not like Thomas. None of us were."

"I think I've kept you around for long enough. You are of no use to me. Which is sad, because I rather liked you."

"Liked me? Liked me? You old hag." His voice rose, snipping off the ends into curt, choppy remarks. "You only liked me because I reminded you of him. Your John. Your Ludington who betrayed you. But we're not him. None of us."

My stomach tightened and knotted around itself. Mother reached out and clawed the air as if her hands wound around someone's throat.

Mr. Connors coughed, then choked back and coughed again. A smiling grimace passed over his face as he dug at his neck.

"Feel familiar?" she asked.

My mind went back to when he coughed and choked at his house, Drake hovering over him. How he said he couldn't say anything about who killed my dad. *She's been torturing him.* A cold vice clenched my insides. "Leave him alone," I screamed. "Stop."

Tiny red circles formed on his neck. Round blood droplets spurted forth as Mother clenched her fingers tighter, her fingers shaking. He gasped once more and fell to the grass, his head thudding off the hard ground.

Cici shrieked and I plastered my palms over my ears again, waiting for the screeching speakers to stop reverberating, all the while staring at Drake's grandfather's limp form. His head faced me, his eyes staring, yellow-tinged and lifeless under the coif of aged eyebrows.

Air whooshed out of me, a withered balloon deflating. I sank to my knees on the warm ground. Salty tears ran into my open mouth. I wiped at my face and tried to stand only to collapse again.

Drake hadn't even given the scene a passing glance. *He could have saved him. He could have.* Except he didn't know who he was. Didn't see his tormented grandfather stand up one last time to save his family. Didn't see how much he loved him.

I raised my fists and slammed them against the invisible glass, except they sliced right through this time. I fell forward, knuckles cracking as they met with the earth. *I'm free. I'm free.* My mind took up the short chant, bouncing the words over in my brain, trying to make sense of them.

A salt canister rolled in front of me. I twisted my neck. Jennie already shook some around her in a circle, the tiny white specks cascading all around her. I tipped open the spout and mimicked her, a white waterfall poured around my feet.

I eyed Mother, now perched on her knees, head cradled in her hands. "What the hell is going on?" I whispered to Jennie.

"She's weak. For now. It broke the spell from me."

"She killed him."

"Who?"

"Drake's grandfather."

Jennie emptied the entire contents. Peaks and valleys of salt encircled her. She gave only a cursory look over at the crumpled body. "What now?" She threw the empty can aside.

"We have to save my mother…and Drake."

"Your mother?" I pointed to the woman on the cross. The woman who sobbed, the chest of her shirt covered in splotches of wet drops. "Ho-ly shit," Jennie said as she took in the scene.

The crowd stood, unblinking, never wavering from their positions. They didn't smile, or applaud now. Their eyes glazed over into pale numbness. "She's got the whole town under a spell. Nobody can help."

A cackle rose from the stage, a deep throaty laugh that melted into hysterical giggles like an ugly wind chime. Mother rose to her feet. "Oh, how I hate when people bring up my John. It just really...pisses me off, you know?"

"You didn't have to kill him," I shouted.

"Oh yes I did. I have to kill them all. I cursed them, hexed them. A blood hex." Her voice dissolved into laughter again. "They'll all end up dead, eventually."

"And my dad?"

Cici's cries cut off, her head swiveling to the old lady. The old woman shrugged and jumped off the stage, landing like a Goth ballerina. "He figured out I wasn't his aunt." Her confident strides headed in a beeline for me. My feet tensed and I had to will them to stay in place. "You're a lot like him. But he tried to kill me, you know?" She pulled the scoop of her dress away from her skin and stared down smiling, then cocked her head again, head tilting to one side like a confused dog. "How would you say it? Hmm. I wasn't havin' that." She snapped her fingers and shifted her hip.

I folded my arms over myself, bold, cocky, wishing to hell the salt would hold up. "That's so ten years ago."

"Well, excuuuse me. That's what being over five-hundred years old does to you. Decades go by like *that*." She snapped her fingers again.

I barely noticed. *Wait. 500 years? That doesn't make sense. The witch burnings here weren't until like the 1600's. 500 years would be the 1500's.* "You're kind of arrogant for someone who can't even do math." Mother stared at me blankly, then her lip twitched. "You said yourself Adams was colonized in 1610. Even if you came over from England, you couldn't be much more than four-hundred years old."

"Please, you think Adams was my first show? I was over a hundred years old by then. I'm ancient. I have the powers of those that came before me. I am strong. It wasn't until Adams when the town burned me that I needed to find another body. It wasn't until Adams that I fell in love and then cursed him when he wronged me. I'm glad I did, too." She played with the skirt of her dress. "I get bored until the heir grows up to produce another heir. That's when I get to have some fun." A cry sounded and I twisted my head to the stage. Drake still knelt before Marlene as she struggled against her captors. "One down." Mother pointed to Mr. Connors' unmoving body. "Another to go." Her eyes lifted to Drake and I followed them. "Pathetic, isn't it? If only John and Thomas had shown such remorse. I may have been lenient." She shrugged and her eyes shone. "But probably not. The whole family line is disgusting."

I dropped my chin to my chest, unwilling to look at Drake until a tiny strand tugged in my brain, saying 'hey stupid, listen to me'. "You can't kill him yet. He doesn't have an heir."

"No kidding. Just when I thought you were going to get it." She shook her head again.

"How are you going to do it? You can't make them…" A lump snowballed in my throat. "…have sex."

"This isn't for them. This is for you and Mommy over there. I put on this whole show for you. And you're the star."

Chapter Thirty-One

Present Day

Relief flooded through me at first, and then a whole swarm of panic. I didn't need to worry about saving Drake. I needed to save myself…and Mom.

"After the running you over bit didn't work, I thought about killing you like I did your father." Mother thrust her hand out at my body, chest height, and turned her fist again and again. *A heart attack.* "But then, Mommy showed up and she just reminded me of something. "A young girl, who I also tried to warn by the way. Next time, don't be where you shouldn't be," she mocked at me, trying to sound like a nice old lady. "Her and her mother burnt together. And I thought, well, it being Past Settler's Day and all, we might as well pay tribute to some past settlers with a little reenactment." She hopped up and down, beaming, her mouth stretching from one side of her face to the other. "Except, the funny part is, the Lynnes that are here won't get to enjoy it."

Mother scanned the crowd. Eyes stared back, following her path. Lynnes? This must have been the girl Jennie told me about. The convicted witch. I watched Mother's eyes roam the crowd. "Now, come on, Lynnes? Step forward." No one did. They gazed at each other shrugging, stupefied, until her head swiveled back to me.

My foot took a step toward Mother without even sending the thought to my brain. I stared down, then slowly trailed my eyes up Rose's blue dress to the scoop collar, all the way to the witch's mischief-taunting eyes. "I'm not a Lynne."

Mother's face lit. "You got it." She clapped her hands again. "How did you know?" She winked. "It doesn't matter who you really are." She opened her arms wide and stared out at the crowd, face bursting in happiness. "It only matters what they think. Or what I make them think."

"Well, let's see, your dad's already gone, I've taken over your aunt's body." She ticked off the people on her fingers one by one. "Your mother…and you, will be burning. That'll take care of your meddling family." She pouted, thrusting her lower lip out. "It's a shame you won't get to see what actually happened all those years ago. But just imagine, while you're reliving Isabella's life, what it would be like to stand by and watch something so horrible happen. Watch innocent people persecuted. By the way, I know my shield's not up anymore…and your little salt didn't work, did it?" She looked down at my leg, the one still frozen a step ahead of the other.

My jaw dropped and I sneered. "Why us? Why make us suffer something so horrible? We're innocent too."

"I tried to help the Lynnes because they didn't get in my way. *You* most certainly have tried to get in my way."

"You're sick."

The old woman smiled, tiny creases splintering her lips. "Hmm. Thank you."

Mother spun around, tapping her chin. "Now, let's see here. What to do? What to do? Both at once? Have the younger one watch? Decisions. Decisions. God, it's so hard planning out a delicious appetizer."

I squirmed in my spot, scared to move. "I thought you couldn't hurt Drake."

"I'm not. He's going to be making an heir today."

My heart accelerated with Mother's words. "What?"

"Well, maybe not exactly today. That will happen in due time, but I'm binding them. You know, so he can't go off and mate with anyone else. Like you, for instance. Twenty-first century men are finicky, sexually charged. Ever since the seventies, I've had to bind the couple together. You never know if one might stray, then I'll have to track down more and more heirs." She waved her hand. "I'm…opposed to doing that." I shook my head, stomach erupting in hot, acidic lava. "After tonight, there will be no one else in Drake's heart but Marlene."

"He said he loved me."

"He probably meant it." Mother Shipton shrugged. "But not after tonight."

My pulse dialed up inside, blood rushing through. I took off at my aunt's body in a flat out run.

Mother's eyes widened. She couldn't do anything else before I tackled her and held her wrists above her head, pinning them to the ground with her hands. Mother bucked underneath, but something had snapped inside. I wanted to take her down, kill her even.

Jennie raced up beside me, chanting, the old school canvas doll in her hand. "I bind you to me, I bind you to me." Her eyes shut tight, she laid a hand on my shoulder and a shock rippled through me. I followed her lead, repeating the chant in the same melodic voice.

"What are you doing? What?" Mother's eyes searched frantically around the park. I twisted. People shook their heads, whispering to each other. They were coming out of their trances.

"There," Jennie said. "She's bound to me."

"Which means?" I asked, still pinning Rose's hands to the grass.

"We can make her do whatever we want."

Mother's bitter laugh rose up through her throat. "You two are stupid."

"Shut u—…Ugh, god." Jennie dropped to her knees, cradling her head with her hands. "Oh god please…"

"What's wrong?" I flipped to Jennie's side as she rolled to her back, her body arching in pain as she tore at her hair. "Jennie?"

Courtney appeared, skipping up next to the threesome and kicked at Jennie with her foot. I glanced up. Courtney's short, pixie hair stuck out in all directions. "Remember me?" She picked up the doll Jennie dropped and knelt before Mother. "Don't worry, Mother. I'll fix this."

"Please," Mother said, disgust tingeing her voice. "I'm fine." She tore the doll from Courtney's hands and threw the wasted spell on the stage. "Just wanted to let the girls think they were getting somewhere."

I rubbed Jennie's shoulders as she still writhed in pain, kicking out, her rubber-soled shoes peeling up grass mounds. "Shh, Jennie. Shh." The more I comforted, the higher her cries got. I pivoted to Mother and Courtney, who smiled down, admiring. "Please, stop this."

Courtney waved her hand over Jennie and closed her fist. Her cries quieted to whimpers. "There."

Mother protested. "She got in my way."

"She's a powerful witch. We'll be able to use her."

Mother shrugged and nudged Jennie's limp forearm with her foot. It fell back into place. She smiled and walked back toward the stage. "Bring the girl, Courtney."

My heart steadied out to an even rhythm by the time Courtney grabbed my elbow. The witch led me to the stage right in front of my mom. I was scared, but willed myself not to show emotion.

The crowd, stone-faced once more, started to chant. A buzz rang through the air. As I got closer to the stage, I stared into my mother's downturned eyes. Eyes reminding me of the ones I drew repeatedly in art class.

The crowd gathered in, including Drake and Marlene. The two guards left them and prepared another cross. This one spiked out of the ground surrounded by hay and dead grass.

No one wavered. As Courtney turned me to face the crowd and stepped back into the semi-circle, she picked up the chant. The words were indecipherable, even if they were English.

I saw everyone I met and then some. To my surprise, the crowd started to cower before me. They were afraid. The witches spelled them to think whatever they wanted them to. Made them believe whatever they wished. I was Isabella. A witch.

Marlene stood out in the crowd in front of me. Her face bloomed red in circled splotches. "Witch!" she cried. She spat at me and a splat hit my shoe. I didn't cower or retaliate, just looked straight ahead toward the growing flames.

Marlene's act spouted other courageous ones.
"Witch!"
"Devil!"
"Burn!"

All the while, the hum continued to get louder, until it pulsed in the air. I could feel it as if the space around me were something physical. The air vibrated.

I stared straight ahead, finding the one face I needed and tried to etch every contour into my mind. Hoping that if this didn't work out, and it seemed as though it wouldn't, I could at least take this memory.

His face was otherwise expressionless, though his eyes were full of hate. The fear Mother implanted into all these brains made them think irrational things. Different times, different beliefs, and the witch transported all these minds back to the 1600's.

I knew when Drake stared at me like that, he wasn't really seeing me, he was seeing an evil spirit. The devil incarnate. The devil himself in a woman's body.

Marlene appeared next to him and grabbed his hand. He smiled at her. I stumbled, but Courtney moved forward, righting me, steadying me.

I arched my chin in the air. The crowd began to silence. Their lively chant now only a murmur. I was actually in the middle of an angry mob of witch hunters.

"Isabella Lynne, you have been convicted of witchcraft, of befriending the devil. Your punishment is to burn, burn away your sins. If you be not a witch, God will save you and allow no harm to come to you. If you are a witch, you will be enveloped in flames and your evil soul will perish along with your lifeless remains." Mother stood out before them, replaying the scene from all those years ago. She was the only witch in that town that should have burned, apparently. Yet, she stood before me now almost 400 years later.

"Do you have anything to say, Isabella?"

I stared, transfixed, at the intertwined fingers of Marlene and Drake. "I am not Isabella. My name is Sarah."

"The evil one has possessed another." Mother sneered as a loud hiss rose from the crowd.

A figure stumbled toward me, bumping me.
Drake.

He spread my palm open and placed something soft in my hand before Courtney shoved him away. I encased the object in my fist. Canvas. Without looking, I knew it was Marlene's doll.

Mother continued to talk. The crowd quieted again. No more hum, no more physical vibrations. I didn't look at anyone else, but I felt a change in the air.

A plan.

Mother motioned to the guards in the costumed brown trousers. "String her up, boys." They nodded in consent.

My hand shot in the air. The canvas doll hung from its arm, dangling before them all.

Mother gasped. "Get that. It's the binding doll."

I ran to the middle of the two crosses, grabbed the torch from its post, and threw it down on the empty cross, the one meant for me. The fire blazed, rearing up, the flames reaching for me. I backpedaled until my foot caught on a root and I tripped, dropping the binding doll at the edge of the hay.

There were no flames there to catch it on fire.

Mrs. Shipton laughed. She took after me at a run, moving quite quickly for an older woman. Before she got to me, I flung myself on my back. The fire was so near, I knew if I went back anymore, I would be immersed in it.

Drake tackled the witch's right leg, leaving her to sprawl out. Rose ended up on top of me. Her elbow slammed into my forehead. I winced, my head pounding.

I kicked out, flailing, hitting Mother in the mouth as adrenaline coursed through me. I flung myself at Rose, forcing myself on top, pinning her hands. I let my entire weight sink into her. A wetness streamed from my forehead and I knew I'd been cut. It started to run off in drips, landing on Rose's exposed neck.

Looking behind me, I found Drake staring at us. Everyone was staring at us. Their eyes were coming back to their own. They twitched and swayed nervously on their feet.

"It's done," I said when Rose started to struggle beneath me. I held her face to the ground with my hand.

"Ha," Mrs. Shipton laughed. "You foolish bitch." Rose's words were muffled, half of her mouth smashed in the dirt.

I saw the object sailing at me from the corner of my eye.

A piece of wood.

Bright orange flames engulfed a smoldering log with red-hot embers. It flew at me. I tried to duck out of the way only to get caught on the shoulder.

My shirt went up in flames. Heat tore through me, boiling my skin. *This bitch can move things with her mind.* I rolled off Rose and kept rolling in the dirt to smother the fire. The pain was excruciating.

Hands patted me, trying to put the flames out.

Drake.

My shirt was singed. The skin underneath resembled one heck of a nasty sunburn and the air smelled funny. But the fighting had lessened the witch's powers. More and more townspeople started to blink, like they were coming out of a trance.

"You okay?" Drake asked. He didn't wait for an answer. He pulled me up and we faced Rose together.

Part of the embers got her too. Tiny burns singed her dress, the edges crispy black.

Drake was the only one who fully snapped out of the spell. The others watched, looking back and forth, like they had no interest either way.

Even though I was burnt and bloody, I was ready to fight. Drake was already in a defensive stance.

"How touching," Rose feigned sympathy.

I spoke up. "You can't hurt him anymore."

"I see that." She eyed Drake's neck. "Black onyx. Protection stone. How'd you figure that out?"

"My grandfather." Drake's face contorted in pain. His grandfather's dead body lay so near. "Your spell weakened as you were gearing up for this…" He opened his hands wide, gesturing all around them. "…show. He wasn't in pain anymore."

I reached out and clutched Drake's hand. I wanted to hold him, to ask him what happened. He squeezed me back and Mother caught the movement. "So, I can't control your mind like I can everyone else." I peeked behind the witch. It was true. Everybody's stare turned blank again, unblinking. "But I can keep you guys apart before I do the binding spell."

Mother thrust her hands out to the side, perpendicular to her body and the hold we had on each other ripped apart. Both of us went flying in opposite directions. I landed on my side, clutching my ribs, my insides burning.

I searched for Drake. He landed on his back. He coughed, like he had the wind temporarily knocked out of him.

"Courtney, bring me the materials for the binding spell." Courtney rushed to the side of the stage and brought back a wooden box.

Mother took out red ribbon, two pictures, and a knife while Courtney ran to get the doll I had dropped. She placed the two pictures facing each other and poked holes around the outside, puncturing the pictures with the tip of the knife and then turning it. "I bind you two to one another. I bind you two to one another." She repeated the same line, while sewing the red ribbon in and out of the puncture holes until she tied off each end around the binding doll.

My face crumpled, salty tears burned the cuts marring my skin. I struggled to get up. I did it too fast and a stab of pain speared my side. "No!"

Too late, Marlene ran to Drake and hovered around him, hugging him.

I stood up now, fueled by rage. I stalked up to the old woman who gleamed down with pride at her spell and I pushed her. I lowered my good shoulder, ignoring the chorus of agonizing stings that ravaged my body, and rammed myself into her back, sending her sprawling toward the fire. The old woman's body stopped, just an inch before the sticks and hay, her hands flailing, trying to recover her balance. I ran at her again and tackled her into the fire.

Oppressive heat smothered me. Flames leapt up all around as I rolled off onto the ground. Mother still screeched within the licking red and orange heat. Her face was contorted into a heaping mess as her skin melted away.

I rolled and kept rolling. My bare arms and legs stung a lot, a hell of a lot. For the most part though, I had used Rose's body as a shield. I stood and watched the fire envelop the old woman, thick black smoke rising above, wafting toward the star filled night.

I limped toward my mother and looked up into her face. Cici smiled down. "My baby," she said. My eyes drooped and I fell into my mother's bramble of sticks.

Chapter Thirty-Two

Present Day

My eyes fluttered open. The light stung, searing my irises. I looked around, dazed, eyes wanting to close on me.

"She'll be okay," an unfamiliar male voice answered an unheard question.

"Do you think she remembers?" His voice. Drake's. I tried to call out to him. Nothing happened. My eyes still fluttered.

"There's no reason that she shouldn't. Her CT scan was negative, but…"

Stay awake! I screamed inside myself.

My eyes blinked closed once more.

****

Visions came and went. I thought I saw Drake a lot. A few times, Cici and Jennie joined him. The old Jennie and the new Cici, but no one joked around like usual. Drake always seemed to be concentrating. Jennie and Cici gestured toward me a lot. Drake just stared at me, concentrating.

****

I started to regain consciousness again. I blinked a couple times. The room was dark and I could tell I wasn't in the hospital anymore. I breathed out in relief.

I slowly opened my eyes, letting them adjust and focus around me.

I turned my head. A bouquet of red roses sat on the nightstand. The door was open at the foot of the bed, letting in a shaft of light and I was swathed in an orange and green patchwork quilt.

I turned my head the other way. Drake sat in a chair reading. This felt oddly comfortable, normal, though something my mind wouldn't let me believe before.

The binding didn't take!

I tried to shift up in bed, and the bedsprings coiled and uncoiled with a metallic creak. Drake lowered the book. "It's okay, don't try to move." He sprung up, his book falling to the floor with a thump. "Can I get you something?"

"Water," I croaked. My shoulder and throat burned slightly. I could look up and see a bandage on my forehead, but I still couldn't stop myself from smiling. *Drake still loves me. He must still love me.*

He walked over to the dresser and poured me a glass from a pitcher. He helped me sit up a little as my dry, cracked lips found the rim of the glass.

I drank. Every gulp tore at my throat, but at least my mouth wasn't dry anymore.

I smiled at him as he lowered the glass. "Thank you." Drake stared at me and then remembered to smile a 'You're welcome'. His face then set into that same look of intense thoughtfulness I became accustomed to in my dream-like state. He must be overwhelmed. "Is everyone okay?" I asked. "My mom?"

"Staying here while she settles everything. I'm afraid you got the worst of it."

"Ain't that always the kicker? Someone goes out of their way to save somebody else and they always get the worst of it." I laughed and Drake seemed surprised. His eyebrow arched, making his forehead wrinkle. *Okay. Not in the mood for joking. Got it.* It's no wonder, though. He probably thought he lost me. I thought I had lost him. More serious now, I asked, "What about you? Are you okay?"

"Actually." Drake looked sheepishly to the floor. "Yeah, I'm doing really well."

A knock sounded on the door that sent my heart into a flip. Drake held up a finger to me. He crossed the creaking wood floor and pulled the door open. I twisted my head. I couldn't see around Drake's body though. His voice low, caressing as his head swooped down.

My heart froze. I sucked in a deep breath. I couldn't seem to get enough air inside me. Drake shut the door and waited, his hand still on the knob before he turned around again. "Hmm. Sorry." He crossed back over to the chair and smiled again, a half smile, a nervous twitchy smile. Not the smile that lined his face when he first met me. Not the smile he gave me so many times after. "This definitely isn't the right time to tell you this, but...Marlene and I are back together. Since she just showed up, I knew you'd be wondering and..." Drake blabbered on, his chair groaning as he shifted positions several times and stared down at his hands where they lay against his thighs.

Oh no. My heart sank. I was sure, since I was here, recovering in Drake's house, that the old witch dying negated the spell. That he must have still loved me. Cared for me. My heart thundered in my chest, a storm of emotion sweeping through me.

"You see," he started again, "after all that happened. It became clear to me that I belong with Marlene." *I'm doing really well.*

Panic coursed through me, and my eyelids closed again.

Too much to bear.
Then, blackness.

ERIN BUTLER

Epilogue

Present Day

I bounded down the steps until they rounded down into the foyer. Since Mom was Rose McCallister's eldest relative, she was the executor and benefactor of all her possessions. We were staying at the old house until we figured out what we wanted to do with our lives. Well, that was what Cici thought. We were actually staying at the house until I could convince her to stay in Adams.

Yesterday, we went to go pick out an urn for the aunt my father loved, and for the aunt I couldn't help but mourn. I didn't want to think that maybe she still lived somewhere inside the body when I pushed Mother Shipton into the flames. I hoped, prayed she hadn't been in there.

It wasn't long after the whole ordeal when I learned that the Aunt Rose I knew pretty much lied about everything. She did know me. Well, the real aunt knew about me. It was Cici's idea to avoid contact with her because of a strange phone call she got from Dad before he died. And since Rose never tried to contact her again, Mom didn't think any more of it.

"Hey, you ready?" Cici waited at the bottom of the stairs, her face solemn, lips tight.

"Yup."

Today, Cici was taking me to the cemetery to see where we would bury our aunt.

Cici peeked over, her sunglasses hiding her eyes, to study me in the passenger seat. She patted my arm lightly over the bandages. I looked up and smiled. "How are you doing, honey? Okay?"

I nodded.

"Alright, we're here." Cici turned the huge Escalade onto a small dirt road leading into an old cemetery. The iron gates were so close to the SUV that I looked down to see if they might scrape against the sides of the vehicle.

Huge trees sprouted up here and there throughout. A mixture of new headstones crowded around very old stones, chipped and flaking, and with barely readable engravings.

Cici pulled over a little, not enough to make a clear roadway, but it was that, or drive over someone's stone. She pointed off to a corner. "Over there," she said.

We got out of the car and walked up. My heartbeat quickened, my temperature jumping about twenty degrees. I gasped when Mom pointed down at the gravestone between us.

David Perkins
Beloved Father and Husband

I fell to my knees, tears spilling over instantly. "Dad? He's buried here?"

"Yes," Cici said.

I turned around. It was as if I stared in the mirror. The sunlight reflected off Mom's wet cheeks. Cici nodded and took a tissue from her purse and dabbed at her face. I placed one hand on the hot stone and closed my eyes.

Footsteps sounded behind us. I tweaked my neck to look around my mom, half hoping for Drake. I always hoped for Drake. Instead, an old man, patches of gray hair standing on end, walked toward us. A pair of suspenders hiked up blue work pants and a sweat stained v-neck cotton shirt was soaked through at the collar. "Hey there," he said.

"Hello," Cici answered.

"I haven't seen you in a while. Did you notice I planted the rose bush like you asked me to, Mrs. Perkins?"

"Yes. Thank you, Frankie. That was very nice. It looks beautiful."

The old man nodded and turned away. I looked into my mother's glistening eyes. A tiny smile formed and then vanished, as if she was afraid, unsure of what to feel.

I stood and threw my arms around her. "Oh, Mom." I broke down in tears too, and we just stood, hugging each other for a while.

There was a lot more I needed to learn apparently. One was Mom. She was a mystery, a riddle.

The other wasn't so much something I needed to learn, it was what I needed to do. And that was release Drake.

Love had to count for something. It wasn't something that could be forced, stolen, or conquered. It strengthened me. It led me to do things I might have never believed possible.

Like trust someone again who I never thought would be worthy. Or risk my life to save someone.

The End

www.erinbutlerbooks.com

ERIN BUTLER

Evernight Teen

www.evernightteen.com

CPSIA information can be obtained at www.ICGtesting.com
Printed in the USA
LVOW13s1458110713

342468LV00001B/158/P